Ray Takeshi
and the
Medallions of Skarth

Ray Takeshi

and the

Medallions of Skarth

J. Boyett

SALTIMBANQUE BOOKS

NEW YORK

Typeset by Christopher Boynton

Saltimbanque Books, New York
www.saltimbanquebooks.com
jboyett.net

ISBN: 978-1-941914-12-0

For Leo and Mary.

For Chris Boyett, Pam Carter, Dawn Drinkwater, and
Andy Shanks.

Acknowledgments

As usual, many thanks to Kelly Kay Griffith for her help with the manuscript.

Ray Takeshi
and the
Medallions of Skarth

One

It wasn't like Ray had any idea about the assassin, the Thrall, the Child Eater, or the rest of it—he just had a funny feeling as he drove by the bus depot, shortly before dawn. A feeling so vague he almost ignored it. But he was just aimlessly driving, burning off steam and burning up gas. He might as well check it out.

He really expected it to be nothing. Ned could talk his bald head blue about Ray's birthright, about how psychically sensitive his long-dead parents had been, about how he had some big destiny to fulfill and one day would take his place in the shadowy struggle against the Dark Forces. But whatever. Ray Takeshi had just about decided that was all a load of bullcrap.

The bus depot gleamed in the glow of the halogen lamps, here on the outskirts of town. It was peaceful and deserted, most notably of buses. Sixteen years old and an aspiring cynic, Ray took a sour, superior pleasure in all evidence of corruption and vice. The new bus depot was a nice example of it. The mayor had gotten elected partly on the promise of revamping the public transportation system. But in a city as small as this one, car dealerships held a lot of clout. So to keep the progressives happy, the municipal government had set aside a few million in the budget for the bus system; to keep the construction companies happy, they'd blown it all on this shiny modernist oasis out among the cow pies; and to keep the dealerships happy, they'd made it harder than ever to actually ride the bus. If you were too poor to own a car, then screw you. If you wanted to take a bus, say, three miles to your job, then you had to walk at least fifteen minutes to the bus stop; wait maybe an hour for the bus; take it all the way outside the city limits to this deserted depot; and wait God knew how long for a so-called "connecting" bus to leave the depot and take you back to the general vicinity of your job.

Not even Ray was too poor for a car, even if his was only a third-hand one that he'd dubbed FrankenHonda, because its blue passenger door didn't match the dark red of the rest of the vehicle.... Except, he reminded himself as he eased FrankenHonda into the empty parking lot, he *was* too poor. It was Ned who'd bought the car, for his birthday almost six months ago. Because he was still mad at Ned (he usually was, these days), it made him burn with shame to owe him any gratitude.

Getting out of the car, locking it behind him, he started to fantasize about how cool it would be if he really did find something amiss, and took care of it himself. Once again he heard replaying in his mind Ned's reproaches from an hour ago: "You've got to concentrate harder on your studies," he'd said. "Why can't you levitate? You ought to be able to do that by now."

"Come on, Ned. Leave me alone."

"You've got to start acting like a man." Ray found it excruciating to have his masculinity questioned by Ned. With his weak chin, narrow shoulders, slight paunch, thinning hair, and reedy voice that turned almost into a whine when exasperated, Ray's guardian was not exactly an action-hero prototype. Sometimes Ray fantasized that his biological father, who had died alongside Ray's mother in sorcerous battle shortly after Ray's birth, had been a mix of Arnold Schwarzenegger's brawn, James Bond's seductive charm, and Toshihiro Mifune's proud courage. This, despite the fact that Ray had seen plenty of photos of his parents and knew that his dad had been an ordinary-looking Japanese guy in glasses, slightly shorter than Ray's blonde, sad-eyed mother.

"The Fates are preparing a test for you," Ned had said. "That's the age you're at. Soon you'll be sent this test, to determine whether you'll be a warrior for the Light, or an agent of Darkness, or just plain dead."

"Dude, what bullshit," had spat Ray. "'The Fates'? Gimme a break. What year do you think this is?"

Ned's face had gotten that sad, tight, creased look that infuriated Ray. "Your parents would be ashamed to hear you talk that way," he'd said. And Ray had stalked out.

The bus depot was like a mall with no stores, customers, or workers. A few soda and candy machines were all that lent color to the silver, gray, and off-white interior. No one sat on the gleaming black plastic benches. The lighting was neutral; not really bright, but not actually dim either. But there were patches of deep shadow, as if the lighting had been poorly planned.

When Ray entered the depot, he was still brooding. Soon, though, he grew distracted. It hadn't been his imagination. Medium-sized sorcery had been wielded here, and recently. Super-recently. Ray couldn't yet discern the nature of the spell, but he could tell where the power had been directed. When he stepped upon a certain section of the well-swept and polished floor, it was as if he met some resistance, as if his feet were sticking momentarily to some invisible gummy residue, like the metaphysical equivalent of a filthy bathroom floor.

He stood still, concentrating. Checked to see if anyone else was in the depot—he didn't see anyone. Clumsily reached out with his second sight. He couldn't spot anyone that way, either, but he had to admit he hadn't been practicing enough, and any moderately powerful mage should be able to cloak himself or herself from him. Trying not to think about how silly he looked, Ray held his hands out over the floor, palms down, closed his eyes, and quivered with concentration. Maybe he could at least sense what sort of spell had been cast here.

With a gasp, he broke off. No luck. He considered calling Ned and asking him to come check it out ... but to hell with that! He'd rather leave it a mystery forever.

Ray swept his gaze around the room; perhaps his mundane senses would detect some clue. And as a matter of fact he did glimpse a dull yellow something about ten yards away, almost hidden at the edge of a bench's shadow.

He walked over and picked it up. It was … a coin? A big coin. A medallion, he supposed. The thing was yellow. Though dull, he thought it might possibly be gold.

But he felt no excitement at having maybe found a hunk of gold. Because no matter what its earthly material might be, he could feel it quivering with something that was not quite life. A great heat smoldered within it; he was only able to handle it without getting burned thanks to all the layers of reality between this mundane world where the thing physically existed, and the immaterial dimension where it had its true home. Its heat was menacing yet seductive. An odor arose from it and tickled at the back of Ray's mind, something pleasant but with a discomfiting twist. Like the charred flesh of a creature it might or might not be advisable to eat.

The feeling Ray got from the heat and the smell took him a second to identify: hate.

He turned the disc over, then over again. On one side was stamped a multi-headed beast whose image he could not quite fix in his mind. On the other side were a series of ideograms, like none he'd ever seen before.

Whatever it was, the medallion had to do with the Dark Forces. Ray didn't need to be a full-fledged mage to know that. Which meant that whatever magical event had left that thaumaturgical residue on the floor and wall probably had to do with the Dark Forces, too. Ray was in over his head; he should take the medallion to Ned (handling it carefully), and see what he thought.

Yet he couldn't help but think again about how cool it would be to solve this mystery on his own. Ned was always bugging him to take responsibility for stuff, right?

Half-forgetting the dangerous thing he held, Ray was already getting lost in a daydream of saving the day, when something moved in the corner of his eye. Startled, he looked up to find that he wasn't alone, after all.

Two

Less than half an hour earlier, Melania von Fleiden had swept into this bus depot, here on the outskirts of this podunk suburban Missouri town. She was cutting it fine, but that was all right. The courier would arrive at its appointed moment. These types of mystical transactions had no wiggle room. Things happened exactly when they were supposed to happen or they didn't happen at all.

Her Thrall was nearby, of course, tugging at her mind. Poor thing. Von Fleiden felt no remorse on behalf of her Thrall. He had sought out this state, and been well-compensated with pleasures—more importantly, remorse would have been beneath her. But she did feel a certain responsibility for his well-being, the way one would for a stray animal one had taken in.

The reason he was trying to get her psychic attention was that he craved violence, and hoped she might turn over this assignment to him. If he did not get to unleash a bit of mayhem now and then, he grew sore as a cow left long unmilked.

Regardless of whether von Fleiden felt a certain sympathy for him, giving him this job was out of the question. Firmly she let him know it; he fell silent, telepathically speaking, with the shadow of a whine that he did not quite dare voice. Taking care of one's pets was well and good, but Melania was working for a special client tonight, and she wouldn't risk letting her Thrall botch things.

She glided across the linoleum with something more than mere grace. The locks and curls of her big, red, wavy hair seemed to sway and float, like the fronds of a crimson undersea plant, or like flames licking in slow motion.

Her skin was pink ivory, her eyes sapphire-blue. Everything she wore was black. A black velvet top held in shape by real whalebone stays, which revealed a bounteous expanse of cleavage and cinched her waist in, exaggerating the voluptuous curves of her hips. A floor-length skirt of something like satin, black. And a black cape with a high collar, thrown over her shoulders, attached by a black chain.

All she needed to do was wait. Her instincts had not failed her—strange, silent vibrations filled the air, out at the very edges of perception. This place might be a shitty bus depot, in everyday terms, but the site was a locus for interdimensional transits. Probably why the developers had been drawn to it as the location for the bus depot, whether they'd realized it or not.

One of those transits was happening now. Von Fleiden held herself still. The courier had come into existence around the corner, and would have to traverse the bus depot before jumping through a hole in reality and onto the next leg of her journey. It was a ritual thing. She'd have to pass by von Fleiden.

As soon as the courier had manifested on this plane, even before she was in sight, von Fleiden's nose twitched: the unmistakable smell of a Child Eater. Von Fleiden hated Child Eaters, with their filthy sanctimony. Looked like this job would be performed for both fun *and* profit.

The Child Eater stink was plain right away. The courier's other scents took a moment to distinguish themselves from the antiseptic, floral miasma of the bus depot's daily cleaning (the bus system might not provide many buses, but it had given employment to a few janitors): stale cigarettes, ammonia, cheap coffee, hairspray.

Then the courier came slapping around the corner in her beige flats. She looked exactly like she smelled, minus the Child Eater part.

Her corporeal form was fiftyish. Her graying blonde hair looked like she'd cut it herself and hadn't combed it since. Too-big eyeglasses whose thick lenses distorted her eyes. A beige flannel calf-length skirt and a matching jacket, with one side of the collar absent-mindedly up. Her white blouse was only half-tucked, and her pearls were fake. You could see her veins through her stockings, and both legs of them had runs.

Under her left arm she clutched a beat-up maroon satchel against her side. No need to ask what was in there. Von Fleiden could feel the medallions' essence radiating. It turned her on.

The courier slowed upon seeing von Fleiden, then stopped.

Von Fleiden tensed herself, ready for the courier to put up a fight. No hint of that, though. Maybe she didn't think she could take von Fleiden. Maybe she just didn't give a damn.

In any case, she didn't grovel. One corner of her mouth turned up in a sneer, and she said, "At the very least I hoped I wouldn't be done in by someone dressed as a whore."

Von Fleiden responded with a sneer of her own. "This was never going to be hard," she said. "But thanks for making it even easier."

A blast of ruby heat from her suddenly outstretched hands slammed the courier into the far wall. She left a smear of hot blood and cooked flesh along the floor, and a charred splatter on the wall. So much for the courier's physical form. On the immaterial plane von Fleiden's attack was yet more savage, and the Child Eater's spirit vanished from all dimensions, like fog on a planet whose sun has just gone nova.

The medallions were unharmed. The maroon satchel had been vaporized, but the coins fell to the floor directly beneath where they had been held by the courier. The shock wave that had propelled the female body across the room had not budged them. Von Fleiden had calibrated her attack so as to insure the medallions came to no harm.

She had her own satchel, a black bag of whatever size and shape she required it to be. She whipped it out of an interior pocket of her cloak and began scooping the medallions into it. None of the corpse's filth had stuck to them, so von Fleiden had no dainty qualms about handling her prize. But the smell of what she'd wrought made her gag: barbecue, burnt hair, melted plastic, a hint of sulphur. She couldn't leave this cooked smeared corpse here—not that she had anything to fear from the police, but a crime scene like this might attract the wrong sort of attention. Really, she ought to summon her Thrall and put him to work cleaning the mess. No buses were scheduled to arrive till well after dawn, so he would have time to do a passable job. And it was safer to use quotidian means, like good old water and a mop. Every time one used sorcery, one risked attracting attention from a passing mage, or simply a Gifted. Or some other entity. Magic had been necessary for eliminating the courier, but the responsible thing now would be to refrain from it as much as possible—at least until she'd delivered the medallions. Who knew what might be keeping an eye peeled for her?

But cleaning the mundane way would take hours, and it stank *now*. Besides, she felt bad for her Thrall. He liked making messes, but hated cleaning them, and he wasn't very good at it. Making him sit out the fun part and then do the grunt work would make her feel like a bad momma.

Anyway, she already had her juices flowing. It was fun to just make shit suddenly happen. With the flash of a hand gesture, she got rid of the mess; it blinked out, all the cooked blood and matted hair and flesh and fabric that had been roasted together. The floor and wall were as pristine as ever.

But as von Fleiden took satisfaction in the immaculate scene, an alarm rang in her mind. Casting about, she realized that exactly the thing she'd thought so unlikely had come to pass. Despite being out here in the middle of nowhere, outside the city limits of a town that was very far from being a thaumaturgical hot spot, someone had nevertheless noticed her little trick.

She focussed in on whoever it was … a male, she thought. Yes, almost certainly. In a car, judging by his speed. Not only had he noticed her, he was approaching.

Try as she might, von Fleiden could not detect much of anything specific about his power, or Gift. Was it hidden, muffled? That might indicate a certain level of skill, and someone with something to hide. Or was it simply raw, unfocused, untrained?

The Thrall was clamoring again in her mind, begging to be given this meat to chew, after having missed the last meal. Von Fleiden reprimanded him silently but sternly. If it seemed that the Thrall would be able to handle whoever or whatever this visitor was, she would be happy to let him do so. But first she would need a closer look, to make sure he wasn't more than the Thrall could take.

And she'd better hide the medallions too, on the off-chance that he was someone or something strong enough to worry about. He might even have been hired by a different party to go after the same prize as her. Quickly she shoved the sack into the shadows under a black row of plastic benches, and slapped a Cloaking Spell over it. No one would be able to see the sack with mortal, mundane eyesight. A mage or sorcerer or someone like that would sense there was something there, but probably wouldn't be able to tell what. If they were strong enough to break von Fleiden's Cloaking Spell, then they'd also be strong enough to give her all sorts of other trouble, too.

In her haste she didn't notice one of the medallions fall from her sack and roll along the floor away from her. Melania von Fleiden had many qualities to recommend her to employers. Scrupulous attention to detail was not among them.

As the newcomer came closer, von Fleiden realized that he was nothing but a boy. That tempted her to hand him over to her Thrall right away, as a treat. But she made herself hold off until she could be sure he was no more than he seemed.

Shouldn't take long to decide. He was entering the depot now, sniffing around the site of the courier's annihilation.

Three

Ray jumped when the figure stepped out of the dark corner, as if from nowhere. Getting a good look at her did nothing to relax him. She was a big buxom redhead in a fucking *cape* and, like, a black velvet bustier or something, which made it almost impossible not to stare into her chest. He felt like his own heart and lungs were being squeezed even more tightly than her incredible hips were, by that sheer black skirt.

"Why, hello," said the strange woman. Her voice was not deep or husky—in fact, it was almost thin and scratchy. But in Ray's ear it sounded like the sexiest voice of all time. It was true that this was a beautiful woman, but any unbiased outside observer would have figured she was positively belching pheromones out of every pore—no one was beautiful enough to provoke Ray's level of sweaty nervousness. But Melania was a succubus and a sex-magic adept. She knew how to attract and hold interest.... Plus, she *was* emitting an unnatural amount of pheromones.

Ray cleared his throat; unsuccessfully, since when he spoke his voice came out clogged, dry, and squeaky: "Uh, hello. Hi."

"I didn't know there was anyone else here. I thought I was all alone."

"Uh, yeah, well I was just.... I mean, I didn't mean to disturb you.... Uh...."

"Oh, no," she said. Somehow she made it seem like she was batting her eyes up at him. But actually she and Ray were about the same height. "I'm happy to see you. It was getting lonely here. I was a little nervous."

"Oh, well, I uh...." Whatever jumble of words had been about to tumble from Ray's mouth jerked to a halt. All the weird phenomena he'd been investigating had been wiped from his mind by the sight of the woman, but now he remembered that she might actually have seen something that could have made her legitimately nervous. "Why? Did something happen to scare you?" He tried to use his manliest tone, as if she needn't be scared any longer, now that he was here.

"Well … there were some flashing lights, and … oh, but you'll think I'm stupid." She turned her eyes down demurely and blushed.

"No, no, I won't," he assured her. Drawing himself up a little, he said, "There's weird stuff out there. Believe me, I know."

It would have been hard to miss the self-important little emphasis he put on "I," or the unspoken invitation to ask a follow-up question. Clearly he was bursting with the desire to tell her something amazing. Von Fleiden indulged him: "Oh?" she said. "You do? How come?"

"Well, I'm a…." Ray broke off, flustered. If he just came out with *I'm a mage,* she was liable to think he was a freak. (Never mind that it wasn't strictly true, yet—he was still only an apprentice mage.) Blushing himself, he veered in a new direction: "Tell me more about these lights."

"Red. Bright red lights. And there … there was a person…."

Ray started. "I thought you said the bus depot was deserted?"

She batted her eyes again. "Well … I guess I should say I *thought* I saw a person. But it must have been my imagination. She couldn't really have been there, because as soon as I saw her … she disappeared."

In her doubt and vulnerability, Ray saw a sudden opportunity. After a second's hesitation, he took it: he reached out and grabbed both her hands in his, playing the role of supportive listener and getting a chance to touch that delicious flesh. So excited he could hardly stand up, he said, "You can trust me. You can tell me anything, and I promise I won't think it's weird or crazy. Because the truth is, I actually have a lot of experience with this kind of stuff." Clearing his throat again, he added, "With *magic,* I mean."

He thought he caught the hint of a repressed smirk on her flawless face. That must be his lack of confidence talking. That lack was exactly why he did so badly with girls—all the YouTube videos on how to pick up women said confidence was key. *"Magic?"* she repeated.

He nodded. "So it's best to tell me what happened. I'm a...." He was on the verge of saying *I'm a professional,* but thank God stopped himself in time. "I'm kind of, like, born to this." He almost added, *It's my birthright,* which was the sort of thing Ned was always telling him. Luckily he remembered in time that that was the sort of thing normal people never said.

The beautiful woman tilted her head and pouted in suspicious amusement. "'Born to this'? What does that mean?"

"It's kind of my birthright." He couldn't think of anything else to say.

This time the amusement playing at the corners of her lips was unmistakable. On the other hand she wasn't turning around and walking away, so maybe she was amused because she thought he was cute. Ray could live with cute.

"I guess I ought to tell you what I saw," she said, a teasing quality to her voice. If Ray had been thinking more clearly, it would have occurred to him that her attitude didn't exactly go with an innocent person who'd encountered the menacing hatred he'd felt moments before, emanating from that medallion. But he wasn't being guided by his brain right now.

She continued: "There was an old, frumpy-looking lady. At least I ... I *guess* it was an old lady. That's what she *looked* like, anyhow. But then there was a bright light and she ... *vaporized....* And the moment before she disappeared, it was as if something else took her place, just for a moment. Something monstrous.... Oh, I know I sound mad...."

"No, no, not at all, seriously." Ray placed a hot moist palm upon her soft rounded shoulder. Swallowing, he made a face like he was concentrating hard on the clues she'd given him.

She watched him closely. So closely that Ray felt even more nervous than before. It seemed like she was waiting to see if he could demonstrate ... *something*. Presumably, the competence necessary to solve this mystery. The truth was Ray had no idea what was going on. It sounded like this beautiful woman had stumbled upon some sort of mystical ambush, and witnessed the destruction of an unearthly being. As for what kind, and why, he had no idea.

Watching him more closely still, she added, "You know, I do remember some details of that monster I thought I saw. It was about ten feet tall, with humped shoulders and skinny arms and big empty eye sockets, and a big round mouth filled with spiky teeth, and it was covered either with thick hairs or else maybe tentacles. And it had a terrible stink. Oh, and no nose.... Of course, I must have imagined the whole thing."

Considering how terrified she must have been, that was a pretty detailed description of a demonic creature that she'd only glimpsed for an instant, as the mortal shell which camouflaged it was burned away. If he'd studied harder in his Demonology Handbook, like Ned was always bugging him to do, he probably would have been able to identify it.

He had to get this woman to Ned. He would have preferred to be alone somewhere with her; but the malevolence in the medallion he'd found was no joke. Kicking himself for all the homework he'd skipped over the years, he said, "I'm not sure what it is you saw. But for right now let's get you out of here...."

There was no mistaking her amusement as she repeated, "You're not sure what it was?"

"Well ... no." Why should it amuse her that he couldn't identify her weird monster? "But listen, I picked up some pretty serious emanations when I first walked in. And I'm afraid that whatever created them might still be nearby."

"Mm, yes. But let's not be in such a rush. It's so cozy and private here. And I believe my friend would like to join us."

"Friend?" Utterly gobsmacked, Ray could only think that the beautiful woman was proposing a threesome. "Wh-what friend? Where is she?"

"'She'?"

The woman arched an eyebrow. Seeing her ironic smile, Ray finally saw what would have been clear from the start, if he'd had any experience with women, and if von Fleiden hadn't been pumping pheromones into the air: She was not chatting with him as a prelude to making wild stinky love right here on the floor.

And if that wasn't her reason for talking to him, what was? And, he suddenly wondered, wouldn't that reason most likely have something to do with the mysterious thaumaturgical event that had just taken place? Which she had witnessed? And which she actually didn't seem all that freaked out by?

Uh-oh.

Now Ray became aware of a certain sparkling aura that surrounded the woman. It was evidence of her own magical nature—she had muffled it during their talk, but had apparently decided to no longer bother. He would have noticed that she was hiding something, if only he hadn't been such a horny little moron. Stepping back, he brought his hands up, ready to conjure a defensive blast. Or to attack, if necessary.

She smiled, as if the gesture were sweet. "I don't think this need be decided between the two of us. Like I said, I have a friend who wants to meet you."

Ray felt a presence enter the depot behind him. Keeping one hand trained on the woman, he swung around nervously to get a look at the newcomer.

His heart sank. *No, definitely not a "she"....*

Four

"What the hell?" stammered Ray, stepping away from the leering, drooling newcomer, and closer to the redheaded woman.

Not that she gave any hint she might shelter him. "Why, that," she said, "is Steve. My Fireman."

"Your *fireman?*" exclaimed Ray, not taking his eyes off the wild-eyed hulk.

"Well. My Thrall, more precisely. Though he used to be a fireman, when I first met him. And I still call him that, since I've always had a fondness for those boys. They're so masculine, aren't they? With their big wet hoses."

He tore his eyes from the advancing figure to flash her a bewildered look. "Your Thrall? What are you talking about?"

"Poor boy. You really don't know much about this world, do you? Considering you were born to it."

Ray turned red.

"He is my Thrall," she explained, "because he has been Enthralled to me by means of my succuboidal powers. He was drawn to me in much the same way I daresay you were—I don't flatter myself, I hope? Only depending on your point of view, he was either more or less lucky than you. For you, at least, are about to be released from all bonds—*all* bonds. But not so, my Fireman. That bodily lust that drove him remains … but he has been changed so that its consummation can only arrive in a very different fashion. Violence is what brings the release he craves—violence against a target of *my* choosing. He must await my pleasure before he may attack. The waiting renders him all the more ferocious when he is allowed his release."

Ray's attention was mainly taken up by the twitchy limbs and the raspy panting of the approaching … man. But he stole another glance at the woman even so. "And you're turning him on me? Why me?"

"One must take care of one's pets," she explained. "And you aren't worth my personal attention."

With that she seemed to literally melt into the shadows.

For a second Ray kept staring at the spot where she'd been. Those last words had stung. But he felt even more shame at the question he'd asked. He hadn't been asking why she'd chosen him for her Thrall's fodder, instead of battling him herself. He'd been asking why she would turn on him, after the connection he had felt they'd made.

Pathetic. Pathetic!

He whipped his gaze back around to face the approaching Thrall. There would be plenty of time to wallow in self-pity after this creature had ripped him apart, eaten the pieces, and shat him out.

The guy had no accoutrements, no big red hat or waterproof slicker, nothing to suggest he had once been a fireman. Unless you counted his glistening, monstrously ripped physique, a funhouse version of the ones in those sexy-fireman calendars.

His torso was bare—he was nude, except for a gray pair of 2Exist undies that he'd sweated through till they were black. His muscles twitched and skittered across one another like coked-out tumors. His thick toes and their overgrown, claw-like nails clenched compulsively, without ever finding purchase on the smooth linoleum. In his right hand he clutched a large axe. Noticing its red handle, it occurred to Ray that, actually, this was a fireman's accoutrement.

What really freaked Ray out was the guy's face. Whatever chemical or magical havoc had been wrought on his muscles, bulging and distorting them, the same mojo had been done to his face. His jaw no longer fit together quite right; his oversized white teeth were clenched. His lips were too thick and dark, and his nose jutted aggressively from his face.

Then there were his eyes, bulging like a frog's. Like the beautiful woman's, they were a perfect sapphire blue; except that the whites were so bloodshot that those sapphire discs seemed afloat in whirlpools of blood. Ray would have doubted the guy could see out of them, except for the fact that they were so clearly fixed upon Ray. And now that jaw unclenched laboriously, and through the rasp of his overexcited heaving breath, the Fireman said, "Ready to lose your cherry, boy?"

Ray backed away. Time to let go of his embarrassment and get serious. He kept his hands up, letting the thaumaturgic charges build up under his palms, feeling the invisible waves prick him. "Listen," he said. "I don't know you but you don't know me, either. If we do this, no one can say for sure how it's gonna go down. So it's in both our best interests to talk things over. Nobody has to get hurt."

The Fireman cackled, a sound like concrete being jackhammered. "Keep talking," said the Fireman in his heavy, rough voice. "I like it when my bitches squeal."

No bargaining with this dude; he was too horny. There was a pretty hefty charge in Ray's palms now, and he thought he might be able to put the guy down for the count right away—then he'd show him who the bitch was. He let loose a blast of crackling blue energy right into the Fireman's face, just as the Thrall leapt at him.

Leapt at him, and broke through Ray's attack like it was water from a garden hose.

Ray landed on his belly, breath knocked out of him. The massive weight of the Fireman on his back didn't let him draw any more air into his lungs, either. With horror, Ray realized the guy was barely even using magic, not directly. Only the brute force of his supernaturally amplified muscles and weight.

He tried to gasp at his foe to get off him, but he didn't have the breath. But then the Fireman took a bit of the weight off, enough for Ray to drag a wheezing gulp of air into his lungs.

"Good," the Fireman rasped into his ear. His breath stank like rotted sausage and stale beer. "Don't wanna suffocate you all at once. Wanna take it nice and slow."

Frantically Ray tried to gather his thoughts. Tried to come up with a plan, instead of thrashing around pointlessly; tried to recall something useful from all those lessons of Ned's that he had only half-listened to.

All that came to mind was the corny, vague stuff. Like, *There may come a time when you have to let go and just believe in yourself. You aren't a very good student, and that could cost you your life one day. But if you ever do find yourself under attack and unable to remember the precise techniques you need, at least know that you have vast wells of power within you. You inherited that from your parents. And that power may come to your rescue someday, if you can just let go and get out of your own way.* Ned had delivered variations on that speech more than once.

Ray could not remember any specific technique that would keep him from getting the shit pounded out of him. It would be great if some sort of power could just arise from deep within him and take care of things. But how could he "just let go" with this maniacal thing on his back?

The Fireman had him in some sort of complex wrestling hold that Ray couldn't have diagrammed, and he could move no part of his body more than an inch or two in any direction. That meant his head was stuck where it was and he could only look in the direction his eyes were already pointing. But that was good enough to see the beautiful redhead, who had unmelted from those shadows, and who was kneeling before a row of black plastic benches. She was messing around with something under one of the seats. A pile of yellow somethings. Medallions, a bunch of them, just like the one he'd found.

The Fireman's large hand shoved itself painfully into the small of Ray's back. Shoved between his back and the Fireman's belly, where there wasn't really room for it. Ray yelped as it crunched over his vertebrae and bore down on his kidneys. The big hand was moving toward his waistband.

"What kind of little girl are you?" The Fireman's hiss was a roar in Ray's ear, like a hurricane wind. "Are you the kind who puts out on a first date?"

Now Ray had an inkling where that hand was going. He tried to shout and buck, but he was too tiny under the Fireman.

The Fireman giggled. "Awesome," he said. "I love it when they know what's coming."

"Don't take all night, Steve," the woman warned.

"You promised!" he shouted, flying into a tantrum. Ray felt hot spittle hit the back of his head. "You *promised* me!"

"You can still kill him!" She sounded exactly like an exasperated mother trying to reason with a child. "Just don't take too long!"

"You *promised* me!" he bellowed. "*Promised* me *promised* me *promised* me!"

Meanwhile, two things were happening.

Firstly, the Fireman was distracted. His anger and attention were briefly directed at his mistress, not his prey. And regardless of how impressive the guy's muscles were, mere corporeal force would not have been enough to hold down a mage for long—even an apprentice mage who didn't study enough. Keeping Ray under control required some degree of mental effort which the Thrall could not spare, since his mistress had left this morsel all to him and wasn't helping him restrain it.

The second thing was that Ray was finding some of that inner strength Ned had told him about. The threat of anal rape apparently made a pretty good spur.

He let out a roar that was more like a screech. The weight on his back disappeared. Something like a beam of solid sunlight had burst from his back, crisping the Fireman and propelling him into the air; he landed several yards away. Not that Ray had any clue what had happened. He hadn't attacked on purpose, exactly—just willed some obscure, powerful instinct into action.

The woman's mouth hung open. "Steve!" she shouted, clambering to her feet. "Steve!"

Ray didn't even have time to feel relief, before an invisible force slammed into his side and sent him plowing along the floor.

Five

For the moment von Fleiden paid no attention to where the snooping boy wound up. Right now all she cared about was that he had, out of the blue, displayed more power than she had imagined possible, and might have mortally wounded her Thrall.

As she scrambled over to Steve (Steve Blevins had once been the name of her Thrall, back in his human days), she was cursing. Not cursing that boy; cursing herself. Even if he had been capable of taking out Steve, there was no way he could have handled *her*. If only she'd supervised her Thrall's feeding, she could have monitored the kid, noticed that incredible swelling of power in time, and intervened before it was too late. Instead she'd been too preoccupied with checking the medallions, to see if they were all still there, and if they had been affected by the Cloaking Spell.

She was at her prone Thrall's side. His spine had snapped, and she could hear his flesh sizzling, layers of fat popping. He was blind, but he could sense her presence; he could no longer speak, but he called to her with his mind: *Mistress.*

It was not an accusation. Not even a plea. Only an affirmation that he was comforted by her presence. Truly, he was her Thrall, body and soul.

She placed her hands on his flesh. It burned her palms. Through his nerves and into his soul she sent her firm assurance that she would not leave him until he was whole.

If she did leave him, it would still be possible to find and destroy that boy before he escaped. But she was a just mistress. She repaid absolute devotion with its proper desserts.

Now it was not merely comfort she was pouring into his charred body, but restorative power and curative energy. Soon the flesh would begin knitting itself together again, and the blisters would smooth themselves out. Skin and muscle tissue would regrow. And the supernatural powers she had bestowed upon him would reassert themselves.

Steve Blevins the mortal had had, for all practical purposes, no innate thaumaturgical powers—of course all humans had a *bit*, but Steve had come awfully darn close to zero. But when von Fleiden had Enthralled him, she had implanted within him a seed of her own power, that it might take root and grow, and that Steve might become a more useful slave to her, and be able to reliably fulfill his need to kill. Because that power had its origin in her own, it was easy for her to locate it inside him now. Once she'd found the root she began to massage it, coax it, prime it. Soon it was swelling and rising, and with the process thus begun von Fleiden was able to step away and let it continue on its own. The hunger she had whetted would spur his soul and body on to make the extra effort to heal so that he could be strong enough to feed it. And you could bet that the first thing he'd want to feast on was going to be the boy who'd deep-fried him.

Well, maybe. But only with adult supervision. Von Fleiden did not plan on leaving her Thrall alone again with that surprising youngster.

Speaking of whom, life would be much simpler if she could just erase him right now. Mentally she cast around to see if he was still in the area, but there was no sign of him. No sign of that car he'd shown up in, either. Von Fleiden must have spent longer than she'd thought patching up the Fireman.

Shit.

As she remotely surveyed the area around the depot, the edges of her psychic vision grew frayed and blurry, her shoulders slumped, and she realized just how much the last half-hour had drained her. Now that she had to nurse her Fireman, she wasn't even sure she had enough juice left to safely get them both out of here, along with the medallions. At full strength she would

26

have had nothing—or, well, very little—to fear, from mystical agents who might have gotten a tip about her assignment, and might have decided to try killing her once she'd nabbed the prize from the Child Eater courier. That possibility was one of the risks of her business. But at her current power level, there were just too many fellow bad actors out there who would have a good chance of taking her.

Even if they didn't kill her, they might wrest the medallions away. If she failed to bring her client his prize, her fate might turn out to be worse than death.

So she would have to leave the damn medallions here till she recovered enough to safely transport them. That would mean something a bit more involved than the Cloaking Spell she'd used to hide them from that neophyte kid. She mustered enough thaumaturgical power to conjure a real Sealing Spell.

It only took about ten seconds. When it was done she opened her eyes and looked at the spot where she knew the cache of medallions was located, under the black plastic bench. They were utterly invisible. It would take a pretty potent mage to even find them, and only a real blockbuster dude would have a prayer of breaking the Seal before it expired in twenty-four hours.

Possibly that kid had such raw power within him, judging from the damage he'd inflicted on her Thrall. But she was willing to bet that, whatever his potential, he hadn't yet learned to tap it at will. The blow he'd struck at Steve had been a fluke, brought on by panic.

Not that she was going to again make the mistake of relying on her assumptions. Maybe she was once more underestimating the kid. Plus there was no telling who he might know. To be safe, she would have to kill him before the spell wore off.

Lost in thought, she failed to notice the stray tabby cat crouched in a dark corner of the depot.

Six

What with his swimmy vision, and sudden fatigue, Ray thought he might wreck the FrankenHonda before getting back within the city limits. At least if he died in a car crash that would spare him the necessity of once more facing that horrific Fireman. Also the humiliation of confessing to Ned how thoroughly he'd screwed up.

Luckily Ned's house was in a quiet suburb (of course, the bulk of Sallisburg was in the quiet suburbs, so that wasn't saying much). He met no traffic out on the dark roads.

Ray lurched the FrankenHonda into the driveway. He slammed on the brakes just in time to keep from ramming into Ned's beat-up, forty-year-old rust-colored pickup truck. Flinging his door open, Ray staggered out of the car and up the porch steps to the front door. He managed to keep standing until he had unlocked the door, then as he opened it he collapsed face-first into the living room.

But the lights were out, and Ned wasn't there to see him, to cry out in alarm and rush to his aid. That probably meant he was downstairs, working. (Mages keep odd hours.)

Ray crawled across the living room to the basement door. He tried to shout but it came out as a croak. One lone halogen light pole stood in the front yard; though it didn't shine directly into the high small window, its cold light provided enough illumination for Ray to see his way. The furniture in the room was second-hand and mismatched, the same stuff that had been here since before he could remember. Books, magazines and pamphlets filled a couple of bookshelves but were also stacked haphazardly on end tables and chairs and the floor. Ned's clay figurines littered the tables and windowsills and the top of his pathetically outdated, boxy TV. The ancient shag carpet had a funky smell, and since Ray was crawling along on his belly he got a bigger noseful than usual.

As usual, the basement door was shut tight. As Ray pushed himself up on his arms high enough to reach the knob, gasping with pain, he felt annoyed at Ned for not leaving the door ajar for once in his life.

He crawled down the basement stairs head-first. Before he was halfway down he could see Ned, standing before the reddish glow of his kiln, examining something. Ned's back was to Ray, and Ray was managing to make his descent in a controlled, and hence not very noisy, way. Still, he thought it odd that Ned didn't hear him at all.

Whatever he was looking at must really be absorbing his attention.

Finally he made enough noise that Ned turned. When he saw Ray he hissed, *"Shit,"* and hurried to help him the rest of the way down. As he lay flat on his back on the basement floor, Ray reflected that Ned seemed not exactly surprised by his state.

Not that Ned knew precisely what was going on. "Do you know who did this?" was his first question.

Ray shook his head. His eyes flicked over to the thing Ned had been so attentively studying: one of his clay figurines, which he'd left on the table near the kiln. Perhaps it had only just been fired in the last couple hours. (Ned could never learn anything from the figurines right away, he had to wait till they cooled.)

Ned was a terramancer. He molded ugly little figurines out of clay (he might be a pretty good mage, but he was a crappy artist), fired them, then gazed at them till he saw the future, or insights into the present's secrets, or occasionally some glint of wisdom. It wasn't glamorous. Ray found Ned's skill at terramancy both impressive and faintly annoying, as if he'd been a great master of the piccolo.

"Did that figurine tell you something about me?"

Ned didn't reply.

As Ned examined his bruises, Ray examined Ned. Growing up with him, he'd always thought of Ned as old, but now he was startled to realize he really *was* getting old. Over the past few years the thin hair atop his egg-shaped head had thinned even more, till his pate was bald. What remained of his black-and-gray hair was allowed to grow just a touch too long. The shaggy look wasn't a fashion statement, just a reflection of the fact that his girlfriend Aisha could only get him to the barber three times a year.

His sallow skin hung a bit loose, flabby at his jawline. There were lines around his hangdog eyes, and at the corners of his droopy lips, just above his nonexistent chin. He'd always had a paunch, sloping shoulders, and spindly limbs. Recently, though, he seemed frailer than before.

Bitterness welled up in Ray. Here he was, scared for his life, up against who knew what. And who did he have to depend on for help? Ned. Not exactly the most dashing figure of a man.

At the same time, he *did* depend on him. Partly out of lifelong habit. But also because there was more to Ned than met the eye.

Fighting off panic, Ray said, "Did that figurine tell you about something bad that's going to happen to me?"

"Relax," said Ned. Mournfully, but he always sounded that way. "Tell me what happened."

Ray did. He left out the bit about the Fireman yanking at his pants. Even without that detail, the story made his face burn with humiliation.

Ned frowned. He could tell Ray was leaving something out. "But what triggered your sudden blast of energy?"

Ray clamped his teeth down stubbornly on the insides of his lips.

Ned could see he didn't want to talk about it. With a comforting pat on the shoulder, he said, "Are you strong enough to sit up?"

"I guess so." He just wanted to wallow there, licking his wounds. But Ned gestured encouragingly, and Ray heaved himself up till he was sitting upright.

It was no big deal. Despite his bruises and contusions most of his damage had been spiritual, and feeling the newfound strength inside him he realized Ned must have been feeding him some of Ned's own energy, to speed his recovery. Besides, that concrete floor was hard and freezing. He was glad to get off it.

Upon Ned's request, Ray handed him the medallion he'd found. Once it was out in the open, the force of its malevolence was so potent that Ray regretted having kept it in his pocket. The thing's influence might give him testicular cancer or something. Ned turned it in his hand, studying both sides, frowning that mournful, worried frown of his.

Ray cleared his throat. "You, uh, you make anything of that?"

"Yes. What do *you* make of it?"

Ray rolled his eyes. "Come on, man, can you please not give me one of your exams right now?!"

"I'm not. I want to know if you've perceived something that maybe got past me. It's like I've told you your whole life, Ray—you're the gifted one. Eventually, you're the one who's going to have to take the lead. I'm your guardian, but that's only because I'm an adult and I've been around long enough to know how the world works. At the end of the day, though, you're going to be by far the stronger mage. You'll be the one calling the shots."

Ray couldn't believe that he had come crawling to Ned for help, *literally*, and now he was getting this same old spiel. "Can you please spare me the pep talk? Just this once?"

Normally that would have been enough. Ned would have sighed, looked disappointed, and moved on. But this time, he continued to gaze sadly at his ward. Finally he said, "Maybe this is the one where you're destined to take over, Ray."

It was too much. Of all the times for Ned to decide that maybe Ray would relent.... "Dude, what do you mean, 'take over'? Like you've ever had me come along on any of your missions! And don't give me any of that corny destiny crap. Anyway, I guarantee, guarantee, *guarantee* you that these are not the people I'm supposed to take on my own. Okay? They're way way stronger than me. Okay? Are you happy? I said it."

Ray had always felt there was an unspoken contract between himself and Ned: Ned would try to get him to do something, and if Ray wanted to get out of it bad enough to basically beg, Ned would take care of it. Now that he had debased himself and denigrated his own capacities, it felt like a betrayal when Ned kept pecking at it. "I never said you'd be on your own," he gently corrected. "Just in the lead."

"Dude, *drop* it." Although he wanted to keep it to himself, Ray felt that if he confessed to Ned the horrible thing that had almost happened to him, Ned would have no choice but to take over. He would see that Ray had already been through more than should ever be required of anybody, and that it was unjust to ask any more of him. "He almost raped me. Okay? That Thrall or Fireman or whatever he is. He almost fucking raped me. So you can take the lead or we can jump in the car and head for Mexico, because I am *done* going toe-to-toe with this guy."

Even after that, Ned just hovered a moment. Was he actually going to keep pressing Ray to take point in this battle? Ray felt real fear at the thought.

But finally Ned squeezed his shoulder. All he said was, "No, my boy. We can't run."

Seven

Ned explained the medallions.

"Explanation" was actually a pretty generous word for it, in Ray's opinion. The clarity of Ned's discourse didn't exactly blow his mind. The medallions were Medallions of Skarth, a sort of currency of evil. In the mundane world, they had hardly any value—being fashioned to serve mean and base purposes, they were made of mean and base materials. (They were gold-colored, but not made of gold, as Ray had thought.) But they were infused with such massive concentrations of spiritual venom, that a daring and unscrupulous party would be able to use them to make "payments to fate." Ray had no clue what that meant. And ever since he'd turned thirteen he'd started losing patience if Ned yapped for too long about "fate" or "destiny" (particularly since half the time he was talking about some arduous, mysterious task that Destiny had planned for Ray). It was like listening to a grown man talk about Santa Claus. Obviously magic was real. But that was no reason to believe in something as cultish and superstitious as Destiny; magic was just a kind of alternative physics, was all.

But Ned was usually right about the basics of what was going on, even if his ideas on their ultimate causes sometimes seemed fishy. Apparently these medallions would enable someone with the right abilities to effect some major damage to the cosmic balance.

"Luckily, they're easy enough to destroy," Ned told him. "We just melt them down." To demonstrate, he tossed the medallion into the kiln.

"The woman who attacked you sounds like Melania von Fleiden," he continued. "She wears a lot of hats, one of which is an assassin's."

"Dude, how do you just *know* this stuff?"

Ned looked at him sadly. "There's a dossier on her in the filing cabinet just outside the bathroom. You're supposed to be studying those dossiers, you know."

"There are a *lot* of those dossiers," muttered Ray. He would have liked to tell Ned that the fact that he had a life prevented him from studying those damn dossiers twenty-four-seven. But since not recognizing von Fleiden had nearly caused him to wind up dead, he held his tongue. Besides, it would be a false excuse. He had no life.

"She's an assassin," Ned repeated. "Also a sex magician, and an occasional succubus." He added these two without looking directly at his ward. Ray blushed. He had futzed over his sudden intense attraction to von Fleiden in his account, giving only vague, confused reasons for why he had chatted with her so long despite the fact that something odd was plainly going on. Ned had filled in the blanks, and was discreetly slipping him an explanation for why he'd acted like an idiot.

"Most likely she was intercepting a courier," continued Ned. "That would explain the surge you felt, that drew you to the bus depot in the first place. Probably what you sensed was her destroying the courier, prior to taking the medallions to deliver to her own employer." Neither Ned nor Ray could have guessed that it was actually the clean-up Ray had sensed. They never did realize their error—not that it mattered. "The creature she described to you, that she claimed to have seen destroyed, sounds like a Child Eater. I bet that's what the courier really was. Von Fleiden probably wanted to include a bit of truth in her story, in case you had been able to identify the destroyed entity by its vibration. Or maybe it was a test, to determine whether you were a trained mage, or just a guy with an innate sensitivity but no experience."

A test which Ray had flunked, he sourly reflected. Of *course* that had been a Child Eater! Why the heck hadn't he recognized it from von Fleiden's description?

"To get something that valuable to her client, she'll need to be at full strength," said Ned. "It sounds like you really hurt that Thrall of hers. If she didn't just abandon him, then she must have used some of her own power to cure him. In that case, the medallions are probably still at the depot, sealed up for safe-keeping while she recuperates. If so, we have until the seal disintegrates to stop her."

"I don't guess we could just, like, let her go?" asked Ray.

Though usually soft-spoken, Ned flashed Ray a look that made him blanch. "I just told you—those medallions could do a lot of evil, in the wrong hands. A *lot.*"

Okay, okay. Ray did feel ashamed of that bit of cowardice. Still, he scowled. "But what makes you so sure she would have wasted time curing her Thrall? Why would she do that? Out of the goodness of her whatever? He's only a slave. Why would she risk pissing off her big demonic client, instead of just taking off?"

Ned shrugged. "Same reason you just happened to be driving by when she released the massive thaumaturgic burst that drew you in, I imagine. The two of you are destined to face off."

Ray didn't reply. He just felt the dread curdle in his belly, coldly. He vastly preferred the idea of Ned facing off with her. It wasn't just cowardice, he insisted to himself. After all, Ned had done this sort of thing before. Multiple times. He was the one who knew what he was doing. Despite appearances, he was the warrior.

Ray asked what exactly they were going to *do* about all this, and Ned said, "First thing is to find out where von Fleiden's staying. So let's go see Britney." At the thought of visiting the Oracle, Ray felt a tingling excitement in his groin.

Just then they heard the rattling whine of Aisha's Nissan hatchback pulling up in the driveway.

They went upstairs to meet her. Ned had a stoical look on his face. When Aisha swept into the living room (she had a house-key, but it didn't matter since Ray hadn't locked the door behind him), he held out both his hands, and she walked straight to him and held them in hers. "I just had a feeling something was wrong," she explained.

"Well," said Ned, equably. "There is."

Ray thought shit must be pretty wrong indeed for Aisha to have gotten a feeling about it, considering that she had no magical abilities, and no more psychic sensitivity than the average joe. He fidgeted while Ned told her the Cliff's Notes version of what was going on. He liked Aisha fine, but Ned's ex Britney the Oracle was sexier. Less comfy, though. Aisha had a pretty face, and Ray was sometimes struck by how luminous and smooth her caramel skin seemed when compared to Ned's yellowish-pink, eczema-prone, loose flesh. But she was too big for Ray's taste, and he found her massive rump disquieting. Plus she treated him like a kid. Not that Britney had ever seemed to pay any attention to him at all; but there was something exciting about the cascade of Britney's ashy-blonde hair, her hard little body, her fire-spitting eyes.

Ned finished the story. As Ray had predicted, once Aisha heard that they were going to visit to the Oracle, her eyes narrowed. "And there isn't any other person you can get your information from," she said.

"No one who's as likely to tell me right away."

"Because she's always so eager to help," said Aisha, sarcastically.

"Not always, but she's the best bet." Aisha tried to pull her hands away, but Ned held them tight. Aisha's flares of jealousy always annoyed Ray—as if Ned would ever cheat on her (for Ray, it was hard to imagine that he would even be able to manage such a feat—his guardian did not exactly strike him as the playboy type—it constantly blew his mind that Ned and the Oracle had once been an item). Ned never seemed bothered by them.

He did seem more serious than usual, though. In a way, that made perfect sense to Ray—he was a big fan of taking Melania von Fleiden and her Fireman super-seriously. Still, it wasn't as if Ned had never left Aisha to go into mystical battle somewhere.

He pulled her in closer to him. Gravely he said, "Aisha. I need to say something to you, before we go."

For the moment Aisha's romantic insecurities seemed to drop away, as she frowned.

Ray was curious to hear what the important thing was that Ned had to tell her. He didn't get to find out. Ned pulled her in close and murmured something in her ear.

Whatever he said, it made Aisha's eyes pop. She jerked back and stared him in the face. "What do you mean, if—!"

"If," Ned interjected, cutting her off. "If. Only if."

Aisha was blinking hard and fast. "I'm not gonna promise that," she declared defiantly. "I'm not going to promise anything like that, because nothing like that is going to happen."

Ned just nodded. "It's okay," he said. "I don't need you to promise. I know I can trust you."

"But Ned—"

He cut short her protest by leaning in and kissing her. Pretty passionately, too. Ray might have spared a moment to be grossed out by the old people slobbering all over each other, if he hadn't been anxious to learn what secret Ned had just shared.

Once they were in Ned's truck, leaving the house behind, Ray asked what it had all been about. But Ned just kept his eyes forward and his hands on the wheel.

"Fine," Ray muttered, prepping to sulk. "*Don't* tell me."

He hadn't even gotten his pout in place when Ned, with uncharacteristic gravity, said, "You sure you don't want to take the lead on this?"

Ray jumped. He trembled at the thought that Ned wouldn't take care of things for him, after all. "I can't do it," he said, in a small voice.

"You can," said Ned. "You must."

Ray no longer offered any pretense of an attitude. "You won't help me?" he said, almost in a whisper.

"Of course I will. That's not the point."

"Next time. I promise. After this I'll study hard and train and next time I'll be really ready."

Ned didn't reply. Looking disappointed but resolved, he turned his eyes back to the road.

Ray breathed out a ragged sigh of relief. Hoping to move the conversation further away from any question of him taking charge against the Fireman, he repeated the earlier question: "But so what did you tell Aisha? That freaked her out so bad?"

Ned didn't answer this time, either. Merely kept his eyes on the road.

Eight

The Oracle lived on the wrong side of the tracks. Her lifestyle probably would have gotten her kicked out of a nicer neighborhood.

They literally drove over train tracks, then past the dilapidated, graffiti-ed houses, and the sullen stares of the locals. Potholes bounced Ned's truck like he'd had hydraulics installed. The dirty looks people gave them didn't bug Ray. He couldn't pretend to be the toughest guy in the world, but he was a relatively competent apprentice mage, at least. He could handle himself in any normal confrontation.

They were still blocks away from Britney's when they saw the first cats. The felines would give the truck a sharp look and then dash off, to report their approach. By the time they got to Britney's the cats were everywhere. A sea of fur roiled in her front yard.

The cats parted for Ned's truck as he slowly pulled it into the driveway. Britney's place was a one-story ranch house that could use a new paint job, with a raised patio out front. Clumps of grass grew here and there in the dry dirt of her yard. As he got out, Ray tried to tickle one of the cats under the chin—he liked cats. But as usual, the cat slunk away before he could touch it. These beasts weren't interested in affection.

They were on the job.

Before they got to the porch steps Britney had already stepped out the front door and was waiting there for them, eyes narrowed and fists on her hips.

Ned gave no sign of noticing anything amiss, though. After all, Ray supposed, this was the look Britney had greeted Ned with every time he'd seen them together. The Oracle might not be Miss Universe, but she was kinda hot, and Ray had never been able to get over the fact that not only had she and Ned dated, but to judge from their body language it had been his drab, balding, weak-chinned, bepaunched guardian who had broken it off.

"Hello, Britney," Ned said.

"Who dresses you?" she snapped. "There's a hole in your T-shirt."

"Can we come in?"

"I already know what you're here for."

That sounded to Ray like the prelude to a "no." But she turned and walked back in without another word, and Ned followed her. Ray did the same.

Inside the house was gloomy. No lamps or overhead lights were on; the only light came in through the windows, but as at Ned's house they were small and high. The curtains were drawn.

She didn't have a lot of furniture, and what there was had been clawed to tatters. Cats were everywhere, dozens of them in the living room alone, coming and going all the time. The house smelled very powerfully of cat: urine, ammonia, the funky fungal reek of cat food. Britney did not invite Ned and Ray to sit; they all stood in the middle of the room, and cats took turns bounding up the Oracle like she was a tree. Each time they did it Ray jumped a little, wondering how they managed to do that without scratching her. If she was listening or speaking to Ned, the cat would wait, impatiently, perched on her shoulder. Finally she would incline her head ever so slightly, and the cat would slip its mouth toward her ear and purr, in a language no human but she could understand.

That was why she was the Oracle. The cats strayed far and wide, and when they came back they murmured to her all they had learned, then went out to reconnoitre again. With their combined knowledge, Britney knew pretty much everything that happened in Sallisburg, and a hell of a lot that happened in the rest of the world.

"You know why we're here," Ned told her.

She gave a quick curt nod. So she knew about his ass-whooping—must have been a stray cat in the vicinity of the bus depot. Face blazing, Ray wondered if that meant she also knew what the Fireman had almost done to him.

"Yeah, I know," she said. "So?"

"So I know you know where von Fleiden and her Thrall are."

"I know where you are, too. How'd you like it if I just told anyone who asked?"

She turned and walked out of the room. Unfazed, Ned followed. Ray trailed after. In the kitchen there were just as many cats and just as little light. Britney wrestled a massive bag of dry cat food out of a cabinet and poured a pile of it into a huge plastic tray resting on the floor. It made a deafening clatter. Before she'd even finished pouring the food, the mound was covered in hungry cats.

Ned replied to her question: "You know there's a difference, Britney."

"I dunno. That von Fleiden, she's never done me any wrong. Seems like the kind of person it'd be fun to grab a beer with."

"You know what she's transporting. All the evil it could do."

"Ah, but she isn't transporting it yet, is she? It's locked up at the bus depot with a Sealing Spell. You and the Boy Wonder here can be there to meet her when the spell winds down. Which will be at 5:32 in the morning, by the way. You don't need me."

Ned stayed patient, yet relentless. "She'll be back at full strength by then, Britney. Her Thrall, too."

Losing patience, Britney flung out her arms. "So be a man, and fight them at full strength then!" She turned her glare on Ray and he took a step back. "*You* be a man, I mean. Mind telling me why Ned should have to wipe your nose for you? I mean, do you even have any idea who your parents were?"

"Yeah," Ray stammered, abashed. Then anger kicked in. "Yeah, I know who they were. But so what? They got killed, didn't they? So why should being their scion automatically make me invulnerable?"

43

"They got killed going up against something a lot tougher than Melania von Fleiden," sneered Britney.

"Britney," Ned interjected. He had a way of saying things. This soft-spoken way, which nevertheless was mysteriously unanswerable.

Though her eyes still seemed hard and dry, they were turning red. "I want no part of what's going to happen if you go there. You're trying to make me tell you something I don't want to tell you."

"It's the right thing to do."

"It isn't."

"It is. I've seen it."

"Have you? In your clay figures?" She wasn't mocking. It was a real question. Even so, she didn't await an answer before turning her glare once more on Ray. "Why can't you just go meet her on your own, if that's your goddam destiny?"

Jesus, did every single person over thirty have to yap about destiny?! "I need help," protested Ray. Bewildered, he wondered what she was so mad about.

Before Britney could retort, Ned lifted a hand to stop her. "He does," he asserted.

The Oracle slumped.

"He does," repeated Ned.

Ray had the distinct impression that something he did not understand was going on. And as usual, no one was going to bother explaining it to him, even though he might be killed during the coming battle. Hey, great.

Britney gave Ned a bitter look. Mouth twisted in misery, she said, "That's how you always win. It doesn't matter how mad I am at you, or how much I'd like to tell you to go to hell. I never can, because you're always on the right side. No matter how much I'd like personally to slug you in the mouth."

Ned didn't say anything.

Britney continued: "But don't count on me to always do the right thing. You know? Your clay figures ever warn you about that?"

Ned didn't reply. Just kept looking at her.

Not meeting his gaze anymore, she muttered, "They're holed up. In Pleasant Hills. You want the address?"

"Please."

"Telling you is against the Code of the Oracle. You know that, right? And you also know you're not going to be able to sneak up on them, right?"

"I know what I'm asking, Britney."

"Fine. Twenty-eight Laurel Drive. That's where von Fleiden is."

"All right," Ned murmured gently. "Thank you, Britney."

"Man, go to hell," she said, and turned to walk away from them, deeper into her house and its sea of cats.

Nine

Ray was quiet and subdued as they got back into Ned's car. He waited to see if Ned would volunteer any insight into what had just happened. Fat chance, but still, you never knew.

Ned kept his watery eyes on the road. Ray noticed that they didn't seem to be headed back home. "Um," he said. "We're not headed over there right *now*, are we? To Pleasant Hills? To face those two?"

Ned looked at him with honest surprise. "Sure," he said. "Why not?"

"No reason," replied Ray glumly.

"Any delay will only give them more time to restore their strength."

Ray couldn't argue with that, so he didn't. He stared out the window at the passing ghetto, concentrating on not letting his fear loosen his bowels.

Once he was sure those were going to remain under control, he turned to Ned again. "Hey," he said, a little timidly. "What was all that back there?"

"All what?" asked Ned, sounding like his thoughts were elsewhere.

"All that, between you and the Oracle. It sounded like there was some tension there."

"Well, we used to be an item, you know."

A moment ago Ray had been feeling timid and deferential because, after all, Ned was about to risk his life fighting foes so as to keep them from murdering Ray. Already, though, he was beginning to itch again with the irritation his guardian customarily inspired in him. "Yes, I *know* that," said Ray. "But I just meant it seemed *different* this time, was all."

At first it seemed like Ned wouldn't reply. Ray was getting ready to roll his eyes and look out the window again when Ned spoke, after all.

"Sometimes people want to fight destiny," he said. "Britney's been around long enough to know better, but still."

Destiny again. Ray's first thought was that this was a veiled critique of his own doubts. But he got a vibe like Ned really was talking about the Oracle. He turned back to his window, still uncertain and nervous, to watch the town roll by.

Ray thought they were going to spend the rest of the trip in silence, but then Ned started talking again. "I know it irritates you to hear this, but you'll be able to prevail on the day you become a man." As always when Ned referred to his impending manhood, Ray curled up inside with embarrassment like a poked roly-poly. "And the path to that manhood lies through love."

That was even more embarrassing, but Ray managed to gape at Ned despite the hot shame fizzing through his blood. "'Love'? I'm supposed to 'love' these people?" The word conjured visions of von Fleiden's rolling curves, and then the memory of the Fireman's monstrous penis knocking at his back door. He blushed so hard that he gasped in pain at so much blood crashing into the flesh of his face.

Ned only shrugged. Was this love stuff something the clay had told him, or just a platitude Ned had felt he ought to pass along? Ray was too disgusted to bother trying to figure it out.

It never really took long to get anywhere in Sallisburg. The place wasn't big enough. That having been said, Pleasant Hills was all the way on the other side of town from the Oracle's crummy hood. They traversed the miniscule downtown, then a few more intervening residential neighborhoods. Downtown was in a little valley, so after passing through it they were climbing onto a higher elevation. Soon they were among the money-sodden and manicured green lawns of Pleasant Hills.

Ray had never hung out here much. Being home-schooled, he had almost no acquaintances his own age, and none of the ones he did have lived up here. Which meant he didn't know the geography of the neighborhood, which meant that when Laurel Avenue leapt out at him he was as startled as a baby by a jack-in-the-box.

He'd been hoping Laurel Avenue would turn out not to exist at all. Or that Ned would get lost. Or that Ned would have a change of heart, drop Ray off someplace safe, and go on and take care of von Fleiden himself, and her Fireman. Ray felt sure that Ned was strong enough a mage to do that, if he wanted to. He'd just decided this would be good for Ray—help him grow as a person, or some bullshit like that.

He watched the numbers blink along the curb, too fast. As they counted down closer and closer to twenty-eight, Ray felt he might literally have a heart attack. Then they were there, the truck bouncing up into the slope of the driveway, approaching the small mansion atop a hill. Ray hoped that there would be a lot of innocent people out in their front yards, families, and Ned would decide for that reason to come up with some plan other than frontal assault. After all, it had only been a little more than three hours since the bus depot battle, they still had almost twenty-one hours till the Sealing Spell expired. But the neighborhood seemed eerily deserted.

Normal people were probably either at school or at work, he remembered. That was how normal folks spent their Wednesdays.

Ned cut the engine and took out the key. "We should have parked a few blocks away and then walked over," Ray reproached him. "Now they'll have heard us. They know we're coming."

"They already do," Ned said mildly, not bothering to look at his ward as he got out of the car. "You know that, Ray."

Yeah, he did. He was trembling as he followed Ned out of the car.

The neighborhood was so quiet that their sneaker soles sounded loud as they climbed the slope of the concrete driveway. In the distance was the wet shushing of a sprinkler. The leaves on the many trees rustled in the air.

"Where are they?" whispered Ray.

"Probably relaxing," opined Ned.

While Ray was still trying to figure out how to sneak into the house, Ned started to walk around it to the back yard. Reaching out with his senses, Ray realized that Ned was right; powerful centers of dark thaumaturgical energy were pulsating back there, centers which were almost certainly nested within the corporeal bodies of their foes. If he hadn't been being such a dopey coward, he would have picked up on it right away. In a spurt of self-loathing he told himself to stop being such a fucking girl and start paying attention.

Despite the fact that those two entities who thrummed so malevolently in the backyard were the last things he wanted to walk toward, he picked up his pace, because he wanted even less to be deprived of Ned's protection. By the time they rounded the corner of the house, Ray was right behind Ned and staring at the back of his bald head. For the first time he noticed that he'd grown about an inch taller than Ned, sometime recently.

There was a pool in the backyard. Melania von Fleiden and her Thrall lounged by its sapphire waters.

The Thrall floated on a pink inflated raft, drifting with a gentle motion that contrasted to the hungry hate of the rictus he fixed upon Ray. The bloated, skin-stretched musculature of his body was scabby, brown, and crimson with burns. Probably for that reason, he was completely nude, glistening with an unguent so reflective it hurt the eyes. The massive veined hook of his penis thrust up in quivering priapism.

It said a lot about the seductive powers of von Fleiden—chemical, magical, and aesthetic—that her form was able to distract Ray from such a sight, and even awaken the stirring of an erection of his own, a sort of junior partner to the Fireman's. The somber fire tones of her hair seemed to laugh darkly at the way they set off the white cream of her flesh. She wore an almost nonexistent bikini; the impossible paleness of her skin was absolutely uniform, and was presumably protected from the solar rays by supernatural means more effective than any suntan lotion. As Ned and Ray appeared, she rose from her poolside lounge chair with a smile. Although she padded alongside the pool on bare feet, from the arch of her back and the fetching muscular tension in her legs and buttocks, one would have thought her to be in high heels.

"Well," she said, her lips pursed into a kissy, contemptuous pout as her gaze slid from Ned to Ray, "I suppose you're not such a big boy after all, if you have to use this poor little bald man as a shield."

Ray's face burned. Absurdly, he wanted to protest that von Fleiden wasn't being fair. Surely she could tell that Ned was the more capable mage. After all, hadn't her Thrall kicked his ass the last time they'd met?... Well, except for at the end there, when Ray had rallied. But that didn't count, since he didn't know how he'd done it.

Ned, of course, didn't react to being called a little bald man. "You shouldn't underestimate the boy," he said.

"Oh, I won't. Not a second time. Lucky for you. It means I'll have to kill you instantaneously, so that I can free myself up for your protegé."

"Don't underestimate me, either. You are engaged upon a dark errand. Renounce it, and I shall allow you to live."

Von Fleiden threw back her head and laughed, her hands planted upon her curvaceous hips. The Fireman emitted a rhythmic grunting that must also have been a laugh. He grabbed his swollen member in his huge fist and jerked it spasmodically, to tide himself over till his mistress unleashed him.

Ned, continuing to speak in a quasi-ritualistic cadence, said, "You are not wholly a dark creature. I can see that. You can break this wicked contract and spare the universe much evil."

"Well spoken," said von Fleiden. "You've done your duty as an Agent of the Light. But with guys like the one I was hired by, you don't break the contract without getting your ass chewed up. You're about to learn how unpleasant that is."

With a flick of her wrist, she sent Ned flying straight up into the air. It happened so fast that, for a startled instant, Ray thought he'd been teleported. He looked up just in time to see

51

the distant speck of his mentor's body, before it came crashing back down at greater than natural speed, as if something were yanking it down. When Ned landed Ray could feel the earth vibrating through the soles of his feet, and the body made a liquid crunching sound.

Ray screamed.

That was a mistake, because suddenly some unseen force was swiftly reeling him in toward the pool. He would have done better to hold his breath before hitting the water. Once submerged, he continued screaming out the rest of his air in a storm of bubbles, before he could think to stop.

Not that it mattered; if he hadn't expelled all the air from his lungs in futile cries, it would nevertheless have been expelled for him by the steel vise of the Fireman's grip. He had dived off his raft to pursue his quarry. His huge arms held Ray in a death grip—Ray was so comparatively tiny that he felt he would have been swallowed up in the Fireman's flesh, if it had had any give to it. The blunt steel hook of his penis was prodding at Ray's back, and the brutish tendrils of his mind were prying at Ray's consciousness. The water blurred his eyesight, but out of his peripheral vision he could just make out the fuzzy form of the Fireman's red eyeball, fixed upon him, and his toothsome rictus, menacingly close to the soft chewy flesh of Ray's cheek.

All that dominated the bulk of his attention. But there was something else he noticed, as well.

Ned was still alive. Despite the epic fall, supernaturally sped-up, Ray could feel his presence outside the pool. The mage was holding his life together inside his broken body, like a child with no glue trying with his hands to hold together a clay pot that's just been shattered. As soon as Ned let go, his essence would spill out of his flesh, and sink forever down into the substrata of Creation.

And he was probably going to let go soon, because von Fleiden was up there pounding him. Somehow Ray's extrasensory perceptions had suddenly grown more powerful than ever before, and he had a pretty clear picture of what was happening outside the pool: von Fleiden was furiously hammering at Ned, to kill him once and for all, fast, so she could concentrate on aiding her Fireman. Ray could feel her rage and frustration at how unexpectedly tenacious the "little bald man's" hold on life was.

But not infinitely tenacious. And she was going at him hard. Ray could not have said where this new sensory capacity had come from, but he trusted it. Ned was up there dying for his sake.

Ray struggled, but that did nothing to allay the pressure squeezing him to death. In fact, he felt how his failed efforts made the Fireman's pleasure grow even stronger against his backside.

His terror of the Fireman was so great that Ray might have gone into a sort of shock, right then and there; his mind might have taken refuge in resigned passivity, in the hope that not putting up any more resistance would hasten death, and its release.

Only thing was, he couldn't help but still sense Ned out there, fighting. Fighting despite the fact that his every bone had been splintered and he was hardly more than a puddle of flesh. Ray could feel von Fleiden's disbelieving rage at the way Ned was able to prevent her from plunging into the pool to help the Fireman finish Ray off. Ray had zero idea how he could escape from the Fireman, much less put him out of commission, drive off von Fleiden, and then somehow rescue Ned. But he had even less idea of how Ned was doing what he was nevertheless doing. There were no excuses.

He renewed his efforts to thrash loose. The Fireman had his oak-tree arms around Ray's chest and biceps, and his huge legs hooked over Ray's, holding them immobile. So all Ray was able to do was shake his head and feet, and thrash his forearms like a wildly sashaying T. Rex.

Something else was happening, though. Something weird.

All sounds were distorted here underwater. But it sounded like something was hissing.

And then, like someone was screaming. He assumed at first that it must be him, until the stabbing panic in his chest reminded him that he had no air to do so with.

He'd made the hissing sound. The water, turning to steam. He'd burned the Fireman again, like he'd done before.

Suddenly the Fireman's grip upon him loosened. Instinctively, Ray tried to gulp in air, which filled his lungs with water and left him worse off than before. Quick as he could he tried to take control of his involuntary flailing, to steer himself away from the Fireman. Too late; the Fireman grabbed for him again, with renewed fury. Via his supernatural senses, he could feel the Fireman's lessened interest in playing, and heightened interest in rending.

The Fireman had hold of him again. But it was not such a thoroughly immobilizing hold as before, just a random grip on Ray's ankle. The Fireman was reeling him in, and it was only a matter of seconds before he was even more disastrously locked down than before. He scrambled for something, anything to fight back with. His hand knocked against something that made the Fireman spasm and recoil. An instant later Ray realized it had been the Thrall's massive penis, and he snatched his hand back in disgust.

But then plunged both hands in again. After all, even the most freakishly powerful man in the cosmos must have at least one vulnerable spot. And if there was a chink in this dude's armor, Ray couldn't afford to be squeamish about taking advantage of it.

He gripped the meaty banana hook and pulled as hard as he could. It took both hands to get a solid grip on the thing, it was so wide. As soon as Ray yanked, the Fireman let out a bubbly howl that was so gratifying, it all but overcame Ray's disgust at touching the penis.

Then Ray was pulling the Fireman all through the water, without knowing how; he wasn't kicking off walls or anything; the force of his own mind was propelling him along, like a bullet or a supersonic penguin, and he was dragging the Fireman after him, caroming him off the concrete walls with force that would have killed an ordinary man, even with water cushioning the blows. Muffled, and nearly drowned out by the screams, were the sounds of concrete breaking and buckling upon the impacts of the Fireman. Also, still, that hissing. And Ray noticed that the water seemed kind of hot.

Just as Ray's blind panic was starting to edge out of the way of the tentatively triumphant realization that he was hurting the Fireman, some new force slalomed into the water. Everything roiled, Ray lost his grip on the dick, it was impossible to say which way was up and which down. If he'd had only mundane senses to rely on, he would have had no idea what was happening. As it was, he could sense that someone new had plunged into the pool.

Von Fleiden.

Did that mean she had finished Ned off?

Ray had no chance to find out, because with her arrival the struggle became even more ferocious. It was only a stroke of luck that the Fireman hadn't killed him already, and Ray could sense how heart-stoppingly more massive the mistress's power was than the Thrall's. On top of everything else, it had been more than a minute since Ray had had air in his lungs, and soon he would be unable to mount even a futile struggle.

Looked like the Fireman might have the same dilemma, though. For he was breaking now for the water surface. Leaving Ray behind for von Fleiden to finish off.

Already he could feel the invisible tendrils of her mind and will poking at the structure of his psyche—she would not use the brute force of her henchman, she would strip him apart from the inside out. It took only the briefest psychic glance for Ray to confirm that he couldn't hope to withstand the kind of power she wielded.

So he didn't even try. With his bodies both astral and corporeal, he clawed his way up toward the surface of the water, clawing psychically at the retreating Fireman. Even managed to yank him back down, before he could break the surface and draw a breath. Maybe there was no way he could kill Melania von Fleiden. But he could have a go at killing her Thrall, or at least hurting him real bad. And that would hurt von Fleiden—

and it was she he wanted to hurt, because he was all but certain she had killed Ned.

Ray dragged the Fireman back down, beating him, burning him, drowning him. His mind's eye saw the little glow of life inside the beast-man, a tiny spark protected by all that fleshly cladding from the surrounding water. Ray grabbed him by the dick and the throat, using his mind as well as his hands, and shook him, getting as much water inside his meat as possible and sloshing it around through all his inner nooks and crannies, to splash and seep and seek out that spark and extinguish it.

Over his shoulder he could feel von Fleiden's outrage. Given her epic power, that should have terrified him. But he didn't give a fuck. This was a suicide mission.

Except she didn't kill him. Instead of delivering the death-blow, she snatched her pet from his grasp. Once again Ray was knocked about in the wild currents of the pool, as water rushed in to fill the hole where two bodies had just vacated.

For half a second Ray drifted, alone, purposeless, disoriented. Then his body realized there was no longer anything to stop him from breathing, and he surged upward. Coughed out a couple lungfuls of water. Then his face was in the sun and his lungs were clawing the new air in and shoveling the old out. All this time, he'd been only a few feet from the surface.

Thanks to his thaumaturgical powers he could have survived a couple minutes longer than the average person underwater. Even he, though, had been approaching the threshold of endurance, and for a few seconds there was no room in his mind for anything but the luxury of breath. Then he remembered Ned; he felt horribly guilty for having failed to think about him, even for a second.

Gasping and spluttering, he forced his limbs into motion and swam for the edge of the pool. Went to check on what had become of Ned.

Ten

What had become of Ned....

His body lay twisted and too flat in the yard. The ground around him had been pushed up by the force of his impact. There were odd bumps in his flesh, and spots where jagged bone shards had shoved their way out of his skin. His left foot was a couple yards away from the rest of him, encased in its bloody shoe, torn loose from the rest of his body. All his teeth had been knocked out. Some littered the front of his shirt. Some were glued by blood to his face.

His eyes remained in their proper place in his skull. That had to be the result of magical effort, though; Ned's orbital bones were shattered, and his eyeballs ought to have slid out of his head. Instead they tracked Ray's movement as he approached.

Ray swallowed back a mouthful of vomit. He tried to force his body to quit trembling. He knelt over his protector, the closest thing to a parent he'd ever known. "Hey," he said, in a gentle and ridiculously optimistic tone. "Just be still. I'll call...." Ray trailed off, trying to think of whom he ought to call. He had been about to say an ambulance, but that wouldn't do any good. They would just be freaked out that the guy wasn't already dead. There might possibly be some mages in the area, but Ray didn't have their numbers.

Ned was shaking his head. It was amazing that he could do that, magic or no. Ray was about to insist he be still, but Ned spoke first, in a rasping voice, lisping because he'd lost his teeth, consonants distorted by swollen lips.

"Not enough time," he whispered. "Took too much out of me, fighting von Fleiden."

Ray understood that he would almost certainly be dead, if Ned hadn't been keeping von Fleiden busy out here. If he'd had to face the combined might of that succubus and her henchman from the first, he'd have been drowned. Or raped into raggedy chunks. "You bought me time," he murmured.

His guardian nodded. "That's my job," he hoarsely whispered. "But now I've got no more time to give. You're on your own."

"No, Ned, I'm sorry...."

"Don't let her deliver those medallions. You must stop her. It's your Destiny."

"Okay. That's cool. I'll never argue again when you talk about my destiny. But the first thing we have to do is get you some help, man...."

"Don't waste time. You haven't got it. And I've got less. Trust me, I know. Nothing you could've done."

Ray's blood went icy. He remembered crawling into the basement this morning. How Ned had been looking at that freshly-fired figurine.

"You knew," he said, awed. "You've known all morning, haven't you? That this was going to happen. That was a figurine of yourself that you fired, and you read the future in it. And you came anyway. For me."

"We all have our destinies. The power in you is untold. Untapped. I can see it, even if you can't. But be careful—von Fleiden can see it now, too. She won't screw around after this."

"Neither will I. But first we have to get you somewhere...."

"That Thrall is the key. Her soft spot. You're untrained. Despite your power, she should be able to kill you, if she concentrates all her strength on the task. But as long as she's sentimental enough to keep defending the Thrall, you've got a chance. It isn't like she can leave him in a safe place while she comes after you. He'll die if he's too far from her influence."

Ray knew that—he knew how an entity like Melania von Fleiden went about Enthralling someone. He'd paid at least that much attention to his lessons. The Fireman's life-force now resided within his Mistress; if he strayed too far from her, he would lose access to it. He would become just another unanimated corpse, rotting a bit more rapidly than most.

"You gotta hang on, Ned," he implored. "I know you think there isn't time, but you gotta let me get you some help. I can't do all this, without you."

"You have to." Ned grimaced, and added, "I wish I'd gotten you to study harder. Now it's too late, and you're under-prepared."

Ned hadn't meant that as a dig. He truly hadn't. And Ray knew it. He knew that Ned really did mean it as a self-criticism of his own performance as a mentor, and that he would have phrased it more gently if he hadn't been *in extremis*. That only made it more gut-wrenching. "You were a great teacher," insisted Ray. "And you're still going to be. We just gotta—"

"*Shut up.*"

Ray fell silent. Ned had never told him to shut up before.

"I am dying," Ned told him. "By rights I should already *be* dead. You have no idea the effort it's taking me to hang on for even these few seconds."

Ray swallowed. "Okay. Okay, Ned. What is it you *do* need from me?"

"I need to know that you can perform this task."

"I…. Okay. Yes. I can."

Some of the tension left Ned as he relaxed down into his agony. "Tell Aisha…." he started to say, but then cast around for how to put whatever it was into words. Finally, he just said, "Never mind." A few seconds later Ray realized that his breathing had stopped and his eyes were dull.

There was no point in checking the mangled corpse for a pulse. If Ned's will wasn't there, brutally forcing life to stay inside the shattered frame, then it was all over.

Ray hung his head and cried, then forced his aching body to its feet, angrily slapping tears off his face. Now that the adrenaline was wearing off, Ray had trouble even looking at Ned's body.

He looked around the yard. Aside from Ned's messy corpse and the impression its impact had made on the ground, other stretches of the yard had also been gouged by Ned's battle with von Fleiden, and there was a weird sullen sucking whine coming from the pool, which must have had something to do with water leaking through the broken concrete interior and soaking the surrounding earth.

Ray wondered about the folks who lived in this house. Were they active players in the Secret World? Or just bankers or venture capitalists who dabbled in demonology and had offered to let von Fleiden and her Thrall house-sit while they were away? Or were they just random people whose home had been taken over by this succubus while they were out of town?

Whatever the case, Ray had no interest in cleaning up the mess for them. He did feel that he ought to arrange a funeral for Ned—he couldn't simply leave the corpse of his mentor, his protector, his guardian, his all-but-father, out here to rot in the moisture of the sprinklers, with their programmed timers, to be munched on by squirrels and other suburban wildlife.

Yet that was exactly what he was going to do. For now, at least. Ned would have wanted him to move his ass and get after that bitch and her Fireman. This final mission would have been more important to Ned than getting a proper send-off. And burying a mage was a time-consuming affair.

He'd come back once it was all over and take care of things then. Assuming Ned was still here. And assuming Ray wasn't dead.

The corpse seemed too horrible to touch. But Ray made himself kneel beside it and touch his lips to its buckled, broken forehead. *Goodbye, Ned;* he sent the thought out into the cosmos.

He forced himself to put his hand into Ned's blood-soaked pants pocket. Miraculously the car keys had not been knocked loose. He headed back to the front yard, and the truck.

Eleven

Sometime during the drive back across town to Ned's house, Ray stopped trembling with shock and began to tremble with fury, instead. As he'd walked from the backyard to the truck, he hadn't been able to stop himself from glancing up fearfully to see if von Fleiden and the Fireman were preparing to swoop down from the sky. Before he got halfway home he was spoiling for them to show, hungry to go up against them again. As if he might make up for having let Ned down, if only he could kill those two brutally enough.

They didn't oblige him. Presumably they were off licking their wounds somewhere; the Fireman had wounds to lick, anyway. Good. But that was nothing compared to what Ray was going to do to him next. To both of them. He was sick of being scared. Time to man up.

But then, as Ned's house came into view, Ray slammed on the brakes and felt all his bravado drain out of him. Not because Melania von Fleiden was lying in wait—there was no sign of her. But because he saw Aisha's car, still in the driveway next to the FrankenHonda.

She had stayed. She'd sensed that Ned was going into danger, and so she had stayed, had waited for him to come back so she could reassure herself he was okay.

Ray could picture himself going up against von Fleiden and the Fireman again. But his brain rebelled at the thought of facing Aisha. Of telling her what had happened to Ned, telling her how his body had been ravaged, how Ray had failed him, and how he'd abandoned his corpse there on the battlefield. There was stuff inside the house that Ray might need for the

61

upcoming fight, but he nevertheless was on the verge of slinking away when Aisha burst out of the front door. Something was glowing with a pale blue light in her hand. She stared around, and her eyes fixed on Ray.

Too late to sneak away. He eased his foot off the brake and slowly moved the truck toward the house. Furiously he blinked to stave off tears. It wasn't *fair* that he should have to be the one to tell Aisha. It wasn't *fair*!

As it turned out, he didn't have to tell her at all, exactly. As the truck slid into the driveway, she ran up to the open driver's-side window. Her eyes darted anxiously around the interior, as if Ned might be hiding somewhere in there. "Where is he?" she demanded.

When Ray didn't answer, but only glared straight ahead with his jaw muscles bunched tight, Aisha brought her hand up over her mouth and started to cry.

Ray jerked the truck into park almost hard enough to break off the gear handle and got out. "I'm gonna avenge him," he growled to Aisha. He stepped past her, hoping that would be enough and he wouldn't have to say any more.

"Ray, wait!" she said, through her tears. "Ned would want me to help you."

"You can't," he said.

He didn't even realize that Aisha had followed him into the house. Visions of carnage blinded him. Slamming shut the cabinet he'd just gotten some dried root of aravon from, he spun around to find Aisha standing behind him in the gloom. For a nutty half-second he assumed it was some enemy, and his body prepped to fight. But her face was visible, even with the lights out, because she was still holding that glowing amulet.

"What is that thing?" he demanded with a frown.

"Ned gave it to me. Just before y'all left. It's how I knew you were out there, just now. It glows when you're nearby. Ned told me that if you were ever in trouble it would help me find you."

Ultimate humiliation: Ned had thought so little of Ray's power, that he'd believed a mere mortal like Aisha might have to rescue him someday. Ray scowled at the amulet. "How could that thing help you find me? It looks like it just glows when it gets close. I don't see anything to, like, indicate what *direction* I might be in, or anything like that."

"I don't know how it's supposed to work, Ray. I assume Ned saw something in the future. Some situation where it's going to come in handy."

Something he'd divined from the future. The same way he'd divined that Ray was going to let him down, let him die, yet had come anyway, to help, to fight his battle for him and keep him alive. Ray spun on his heel before Aisha could see his tears, and headed for Ned's room to continue gearing up.

Aisha followed him. "Hey!" she insisted.

Ray would have liked to tell her to leave him alone; he had a lot of prep work to do, both in terms of practical tasks and in terms of psyching himself up. But underneath his angry pain he recognized that Aisha had lost Ned, too. He paused and turned, forcing himself to be patient. "Yes?" he said.

Aisha stared at him. "What are you doing?" she asked. "You look to me like a chicken with his head cut off. Why don't you sit down a minute?"

So much for all that grown-up patience he'd been so proud of a second ago. Stifling another flare-up of temper, he said, "I don't want to let it sink in. And I haven't got a minute."

She didn't respond aloud. But he had to reply to the mournful, worried, inquisitive look she gave him.

"I'm going to get them," he explained. "For what they did to Ned." The words embarrassed him, as if he were being too big for his britches. "I'm going to kill them," he said, with renewed vigor, looking into her eyes. "I promise you. They're as good as dead."

Not only did this promise fail to awaken joy or comfort in Aisha's face—it pushed it into a grimace of distaste, as if Ray had, uninvited, shared some intimate sexual fantasy. Without any of the tenderness that Ray felt he deserved, or any of the grief Ned deserved, she asked, "How are you going to do that? I mean, what's changed from this afternoon?"

"*I've* changed," he growled, and once again turned to head for Ned's room.

She pursued him. "Ray, you need to stop and think. You can't have had time to come up with a plan...."

"The plan is to kick the shit out of those assholes! Anyway, it's got to be done by dawn, when her Sealing Spell expires."

"Then you've got till dawn to think!" Ray ignored her as he rifled through Ned's old armoire, stuffing charms and potions into a nylon backpack. "Do you even know how to find these people?"

Gritting his teeth, Ray reflected that he had a good idea where to start looking—the Oracle.

He was on his knees, going through the bottom drawer. Aisha hovered over him. "Ray, you have to wait. Ned asked me to look after you—it was his last request."

"You weren't there for his last request—I was. He asked me to stop Melania von Fleiden and her Thrall." He slammed shut the drawer and stood up. The backpack was stuffed full of charms, packets of mystical powder, fetishes, and a few potions in shatter-proof plastic vials.

Aisha hounded him on his way back to the front door. "He died to save your life! You don't have the right to just throw it away!"

That reproach jabbed too hard at the sore place in his soul. "Leave me alone!" he barked. "You don't even know what you're talking about! This is mage stuff!"

Without looking at her, he stalked out of the house and past Ned's truck to his own FrankenHonda.

Aisha stopped following him, and stood in the doorway silently.

Seething, still averting his eyes from the house in case Aisha stepped outside to call him back, he got his car started. Luckily the engine gave him no trouble. If it had coughed and sputtered today the way it sometimes did, he would have ... well, he didn't know what he would have done. Thrown a fit, probably.

Though he was seething, it really wasn't Aisha he was mad at. It was himself. He'd told Aisha this was about mage stuff, but really it was about *man* stuff. Ned had died because Ray hadn't been enough of a man to handle his own shit. That was what needed fixing. And he couldn't see how a woman could help with that.

Twelve

On the way back to the Oracle's he tried to run down a few cats. They jumped out of the way and hissed.

Trauma and shame had knocked his time sense out of whack. On the one hand it felt like a lifetime had passed since he and Ned had visited Britney and gotten the address from her. On the other, the déja vu was so powerful that he almost felt like he was still on the same drive; he kept expecting to slide his eyes over and see his guardian sitting beside him, not dead. It had been less than two hours since their visit. At least his clothes were almost dry again, after being soaked in the pool.

Britney must have known he was coming, but this time she didn't come out to meet him. Maybe he by himself didn't rate the sort of ceremony that Ned had. As he got out of the car he slammed the driver's-side door shut, like an announcement. A dozen cats watched him, alert. The rest kept milling about their business.

He marched up the sagging wooden porch steps. He was pissed that her front door was wide open, because he'd planned to burst in, or pound on it if it was locked. "Britney!" he shouted. It was meant to be a roar, but his voice sounded infuriatingly thin in his own ears.

Britney poked her head out of the kitchen. Perched on her shoulder was a gray tom whose left eye had years ago been clawed out and scarred over. She was opening a can of cat food. "In a minute," she muttered, and pulled her head back in.

Ray marched to the kitchen and stood in the doorway, gripping the frame with both hands, glaring down at her as she bent over to scoop the wet food into a bowl. Hungry cats circled everywhere on the dirty linoleum. No way was that single can going to satisfy them. "You knew they would kill him!" he shouted.

He'd meant to throw the accusation down like a gauntlet, then watch her freeze with horror. Instead she only flinched. Then stood back up and walked past him out of the kitchen. "Of course I did," she scoffed. "Obviously." Ray remained a moment in the kitchen, open-mouthed. Before he could recover from the shock and follow her, he noticed that the single can of food wasn't meant to be shared among all the cats—the other felines gave a wide berth to the one-eyed tom. He was the only one who ate from the dish. That one-eyed tom must have been one bad motherfucker.

Ray pursued Britney back into the living room. "Hey!" he shouted. She kept on about her mysterious, banal business. "Hey! You think you're just gonna walk away from me?"

He had followed her into the hallway that ran off from the living room. On the dirty carpet of the hallway was a very long, low, purple plastic trough. Next to the trough was a jumbo bag of dry cat food. To look at the Oracle one wouldn't have thought her capable of picking it up (the bag was over half as big as she was), but she heaved it into her arms and tilted it down so the brown funky-smelling pellets could crash into the trough. Cats rushed in from everywhere.

Just as Ray was starting to hate himself for standing there and docilely letting her ignore him, she dropped the nearly-empty bag back in its spot, straightened up, brushed a wiry hair out of her eyes, and stepped past him.

He grabbed her by the upper arm and spun her back around.

Startled, she looked down at his hand gripping her, then up into his eyes. She laughed.

"Shut the fuck up!" he shouted. "Stop laughing at me!"

She shook loose from him and continued walking back to the living room.

Ray tried to follow her, but all these damn cats were underfoot. He was sure they were doing it on purpose. "You sent Ned to die because you've always wanted to get back at him for dumping you!"

Again, she laughed. This laugh had just enough bitterness in it that Ray thought he had hit a nerve. Good.

"Admit it." He was looming over her in the dim living room. She was squatting down again. There was a low shelf protruding from the wall, with a blanket hanging off it; she flung the blanket out of the way to reveal more jumbo bags of dry cat food. This brand was called Science Diet. As she wrestled one out of its nook, Ray kept at her: "Admit that's why you gave him the address."

"You know, this bag is heavy. A gentleman would give me a hand."

"Admit that's why."

She tore the bag open, then looked up at him, with an expression more tired than ever. "You were here. You know I didn't want to give him that address. Ned knew the score. He died for your sake. You have the power to defeat von Fleiden and her flunky. It's your destiny to do so, your final test. Anyway, that's what he thought—don't ask me, I don't read the future, I just spy on the present. Basically, he died because you wouldn't step up."

"Tell me where to find that bitch and her Thrall."

"I don't think so. You're not up for it."

"Ned thought I was."

"Yeah, well, Ned took a generous view of people."

"You're gonna tell me where they are."

"Oh, I am, am I?"

He grabbed for her throat. "Bitch, you're gonna tell me where to find von Fleiden!"

Later, lying in the dark in his bed and unable to sleep, he would perform countless post-ops of this attack, tabulating all the things he had done wrong. Really there was no need for a detailed analysis, because the biggest mistake had been the first: he had used no thaumaturgy. He'd been so furious that he had lashed out with the easiest weapon to hand, his mere corporeal body. Now, it might be true that Ray hadn't yet learned to harness enough power to enter the ranks of master mages. But the Oracle didn't have much raw thaumaturgy at all. What mainly protected her was her usefulness to all parties, be they Light or Dark. If he had gone after her with an all-out magic attack, he might not have killed her, but he could have done some damage.

But it was for the best that he hadn't. Attacking her had been a dick move, and he was lucky he'd failed. Although he could have wished for it to turn out a bit more pleasantly.

The Oracle tried to slap him off. Then she jammed her hand into the bag of Science Diet. Ray wasn't really choking her—just kind of shaking her—so she had plenty of air to cry out something. Ray didn't recognize the language, but there was a strange amplified quality to her voice which implied she was working some sort of spell.

Uh-oh, thought Ray.

The Oracle brought up a handful of food pellets and flung them into his face. It took Ray a moment to realize that they didn't bounce off, but stuck to him. He had a bad feeling about that.

While he was still trying to bat the food pellets off his face, the Oracle uttered another strange phrase in that odd voice. And suddenly the cats were all over him.

Glued to him. Smothering him. Weighing him down, pulling him off-balance so that he toppled to the floor and rolled around like a fool. They weren't clawing or biting; the warding spell Ray had flung up in panicked haste must be keeping the animals from drawing much blood. Or maybe the Oracle had ordered them not to shred him, for reasons of her own. He wheezed, struggling to breathe through the layers of fur and flesh. Even if he couldn't at will tap the level of power he'd need to vaporize von Fleiden and her Fireman, he ought to have been able to get these cats off him, and he frantically tried to figure out why he couldn't. The cats must be plugged into some kind of massive thaumaturgical net, was all he could figure. All cats hummed with a low level of magic. If all the vibrations of all the cats within twenty square miles or so were calibrated just right, then the result would be a force massive enough to give even a fully-developed mage a run for his money. As for a slacker who never finished his homework, like Ray, they could definitely overwhelm him. Obviously, such a web of vibrationally-calibrated felines would never occur naturally. There would have to be a pretty smart human guiding the process. Like, say, Britney.

Ray was too busy writhing under the cats, struggling for air and yanking at the yowling beasts' fur in the hopes of flinging them off, for him to feel abashed, exactly. But even there in the heat of everything he felt something close to it. He'd learned enough about Britney, from listening to Ned and from his own mystical senses, to know that his raw personal powers outmatched hers. He hadn't stopped to consider that her experience and expertise might have given her weapons he didn't know how to consider.

Well, he had learned his lesson now. Just as he feared he might really drown in fur, after having escaped drowning in water only a brief time ago, he finally managed to pull first one, then another cat off his face. His power must finally be forcing back their spell, or else Britney was calling them off.

Ray struggled to his feet, tossing cats left and right. They began to drop away of their own accord. He staggered across the room, blindly groping in what he hoped was the direction of the front door, hacking, trying to cough out the fur he'd ingested. His face and arms stung from the light scratches he'd endured.

He didn't turn back. Just kept running till he was back in the FrankenHonda, then peeled out in reverse. Cats scattered out of his way.

Thirteen

He drove the FrankenHonda way out on a country highway, then pulled it off the road. He eased as far as he dared behind the trees and underbrush; the FrankenHonda was no offroad vehicle, and he was afraid of it getting stuck. But he wanted to hide as much as possible, in case von Fleiden and the Fireman were out looking for him.

Regardless of how he tried to goad himself to stay awake and in motion, there was no way he could keep going without rest. Since last night he had been subjected to two savage beatings, plus the attack of the cats … and, more exhausting than all that, the loss of Ned, and the thought of all that grief awaiting him, which he hadn't had time to feel yet.

He reclined his seat back (as far as it would go, anyway—the FrankenHonda was no luxury vehicle, either), and closed his eyes. Eighteen hours or so till the Sealing Spell expired. The car was only partially shaded, and heavy warm sun rays leaned on his eyelids. He tried to zen out and ignore them.

Zenning out must have worked, because pretty soon he felt himself slipping into a doze.

Before he dropped out of consciousness, he thought with a fearful tremor of his adversaries: of the immense power of von Fleiden, and how poor Ned had looked once she was done with him; of the Fireman's terrifying, huge penis, and the way his hard blunt fingers had felt as they'd invaded Ray's waistband; he fought down the urge to vomit at the memory of how he'd actually grabbed that huge penis in his hands and yanked on it. A small, dark part of himself hoped that they might find him and kill him while he slept, so that he would never have to know about it. Being confronted with such a wish sparked hot tears of shame. He was such a little bitch, and the only way he was ever going to stop being a bitch was if he manned up and annihilated these two and made up for letting Ned down. And if he got himself killed in the process, fine. The sooner the better. Get it over with.

He thought the shame and the bitchy baby crying would keep him awake. But no. His descent continued, until soon he didn't even remember he was in the car.

Where was he, instead? Some ambiguous, flickering space. The bright artificial light of a waiting room. If there were windows here, he couldn't see them. Seated across from him, on a plastic bench like the one he sat on, was a couple who looked familiar but whom he couldn't quite place. An Asian guy and a blonde woman in black-framed hipster glasses.

"Hello, son," said the Asian guy.

"Shit," said Ray, awkwardly. "You guys are my parents."

"No," said the blonde, consolingly, leaning forward a bit. Her legs were crossed. She was wearing cargo shorts and a Rage Against the Machine T-shirt, had a nose stud, and looked like a stereotypical nineties skater chick. "Your parents are dead. If I were your real mother, I'd be rushing to take you in my arms. We're just figments of your imagination. You're dreaming."

"Oh," said Ray, a little disappointed. But also relieved; it would be weird if his parents rose from the dead while he had all this other stuff to figure out.

His dream dad was frowning. "What do you mean?" he said to his dream-wife. "I feel like we're really here and this is really us. I think he's having a vision."

"Oh, please," she said.

His dream-dad tabled the issue. "Anyway, son. The point is that you've got a serious problem. And we just want to make sure you've got a plan for dealing with it."

"Is it cool if we talk about something else? I mean, my whole life I've wanted to hang out with you guys. Maybe we could use this visit to kind of help me forget my troubles for a minute?"

"We'll have plenty of time to hang out in the afterlife," said his dream-dad. "Which will be soon, if you insist on going off half-cocked."

"There's really an afterlife?" asked Ray, fascinated.

"We don't know, any more than you do," said his dream-mom. "Remember, we're your dream. Not actual phantoms returned from the shadowlands. We don't have access to any knowledge that doesn't already reside within you."

His dream-dad glanced at his dream-mom with annoyance. "I think I can safely say that yes, there is an afterlife. I remember it just fine, so I'm not sure what's going on with your mother. I mean, we just came from there."

"Is this really what we should be focusing on with Ray?"

"You said I shouldn't go off half-cocked?" Ray decided to assume for the moment that these really were the shades of his parents, in the hope that they might bring wisdom from beyond the grave. "What about what I *should* do, though? There's a deadline coming up."

"There's something you've missed," his dream-dad urged him. "A piece of the puzzle. Something that you've been told, but whose significance you haven't grasped."

"Can't you just tell me what it is?"

"We can't," explained his dream-mom apologetically. "Remember, we're only elements from your subconscious. We don't know anything you don't know already. So you have to search for these answers yourself."

"We're *not* elements of his subconscious!" exclaimed his dream-dad. "We're visitors from beyond the pale! Jesus! The reason we can't just tell him what's what is because finding that out on his own is a major part of his coming of age."

To his dream-mom, Ray said, "But if all you guys are doing is repeating back to me stuff I subconsciously know … well, I mean, then *I* must know what the thing is that I noticed, without noticing that I noticed it. So why can't you guys, as avatars of my subconscious, just explain the whole thing to me?"

"Because it's *not* something you already know," said his dream-dad, "because we're not a dream or elements of your subconscious—we're actual, legit visitors from beyond the grave. You see? Your mother's theory doesn't make any sense."

"So there's something I supposedly know, but you can't tell me what it is. How does that do me any good? I don't care whether you can't tell me because of some 'rules,' or because you don't actually know yourself because you're just me, talking to myself. What difference does it make?"

His dream-dad looked offended. "It makes a difference to *us* whether we're really here or just being imagined by you. It ought to make a difference to you, too. I mean, we're your parents, Ray."

His dream-mom put a hand on his dream-dad's forearm. "Let's not make this about us."

"According to you, there isn't even an 'us.'"

"Can you guys actually tell me anything?" said Ray.

"We've already told you that there's something you've missed," replied his dream-dad. "That in itself is an important piece of information, son."

Technically, Ray supposed that was true. "Thanks," he said, trying to be gracious.

His dream-mom leaned even closer toward him. It looked like she was on the verge of falling out of her chair, yet she still wouldn't reach out with her hand and touch him. Maybe she couldn't, because she wasn't real. She said, "Ray. Just believe in yourself. Relax. I know that's a corny thing to say, but the key to becoming a great warrior is to feel the joy of battle, and you can't get to that if you're all wound up. Remember, this is your last step on the way to becoming a grown-up. Your father and I both believe in you, we know you can do it."

Ray was blinking hard to push back the tears; he was such a weepy wuss today. "I wish I'd ever gotten to meet you guys in real life. I wish you could be with me now."

"We'll always be with you," his dream-mom told him. "As long as you live, we'll be right here. Inside you."

His dream-dad threw up his hands. "What are you *telling* him?! We don't live *inside* him, we live in the *afterlife*! We just came from there, and now we're about to go back!"

It occurred to Ray to ask them if Ned was there with them, and if he could say hello (either to the actual spirit, or the figment). But the ambiguous space was suddenly becoming even more ambiguous, and the forms of his dream-parents were growing fluid and blurred. He cried out to them, but they didn't respond—only stared at him—they didn't seem any further away, exactly, but it was as if some new barrier had appeared between them, some sheet of frozen space-time—they looked out at him through that barrier, a little sadly, but calmly, and quietly. There was something stately and uncanny about them. Then their forms started to fluctuate and darken more and more, until the barrier unfroze and rippled as if someone had tossed a stone into it, and then it was all shadows and then sunlight as Ray woke up.

He blinked in the sunlight. Not that it was so bright—it was a heck of a lot dimmer than when he'd gone to sleep. Time was passing. The stiffness of his body told him he'd slept way longer than planned.

So the showdown was coming up. And his parents had (or possibly had not) traveled from beyond the grave to tell him that there was a way for him to win, something right in front of him, something someone had already told him, but that he was too boneheaded to see it.

Great.

Fourteen

For a while he sat in the car. Thought it over.

At the prospect of going back to the house and seeing Aisha, his face burned. He was sure she'd be waiting there, to hear what had happened. It would be way easier to face her once he had avenged Ned. After having been such a dick, he needed to do something to prove himself before he could look her in the eyes.

Ray considered his dream-parents' claim. Had he been told something that could save him? Possibly the dream really had been a vision from beyond the grave, as his dream-dad had insisted. Even if it was only a message from his own subconscious, as his dream-mom had claimed, that could be important. But it seemed even more reasonable to assume that it had just been a dream, one that he could safely ignore. Just a dream some kid had had about his dead mommy and daddy, right before it was time for him to die himself.

He started the FrankenHonda and eased it out of the woods and back onto the highway. Jutting branches made squeaking screeches as they scraped against the door, and he winced at the thought of how the paint was being scratched. Then he wondered what the fuck was wrong with him. How could that be something he worried about, at a moment like this? Besides, as if the FrankenHonda had some kind of pristine paint job, anyway.

No traffic on the road. The woods were pretty, albeit not epic. The late-afternoon sunlight had a muted, refined quality. The prettiness of the light and the scenery was lost on Ray. Normally he would zip along such an empty road, but without noticing he had dropped below the speed limit. Must not have really wanted to get to where he was going.

Something flickered. Sort of up in the top left-hand quadrant of his fly-specked windshield. In the sky.

He didn't even know why he was paying it any mind. Probably nothing but a bird. Except it was just hovering there without moving—so, okay, it was a helicopter....

Shit, no! It was Melania von Fleiden! Flying around up there!

Got you, bitch, he snarled to himself. Now he slammed on the accelerator, determined to get as close as he could before she darted off again.

If he could get his hands on her now, while she was still tuckered out from the beating she'd given Ned, maybe he could do the job on his own. He could face Aisha as a hero, instead of a shame-faced boy.

Of course, it was not lost on Ray that von Fleiden had managed to utterly crush Ned, who was stronger than him, and she hadn't been at full strength then, either. But he shoved aside such cowardly thoughts. The thrashing she'd given Ned simply had to have taken a toll on her. No way could she do something like that twice in one day.

He knew that he was crazy to be racing after her like this. Better to die, though, than to be once more proven a pussy. As von Fleiden stopped hovering and began moving to the west, over the trees, Ray slammed on the brakes and made a deal with himself—if he could levitate and fly after her, that would be proof that he'd advanced far enough to have at least a chance. If not, well, she would get away and it would be a moot point.

He leapt out of the car and tore through the underbrush, straining with invisible, metaphysical muscles toward the sky. He was close, he knew it—he could feel his chakras fizzing—he forced himself to think of Ned, of all that he owed him, and all of a sudden he felt his feet kicking against nothing, racing through thin air.

Hey, he'd done it! He was flying! Not knowing quite how he did it, he oriented himself in von Fleiden's direction and pushed himself after her. As far as he could tell, she hadn't noticed him. He focused his glare on her and tried not to look down or think about how far the drop was.

So far, there was no sign von Fleiden had noticed him. Until there was—she came to a halt and rotated in mid-air to turn and leer at him. She'd known all along he was there, and had appeared in order to lure him into a trap. Duh.

She hovered in mid-air, hands on her hips. Head back and laughing at him, though he couldn't hear it over the roaring wind. He ground his teeth and bore straight at her, dreaming of smashing her like she'd done Ned.

Except that was just what she wanted. Suddenly he realized she was laughing on purpose, to goad him into taking her on now, before he'd learned to access his power reliably enough to be a threat.

Right now he was so pissed that he wouldn't even give a shit if he died trying to take her out. But that would mean failing at the mission he'd promised Ned to fulfill.

He remembered what Ned had told him: the Thrall was the key. He pulled off just before reaching von Fleiden and made a psychic sweep of the terrain below. There—he could sense that fucking Fireman. He'd die if he strayed too far from his mistress, so it wasn't like she could tuck him away in a safe place.

He directed his attack straight down at that son of a bitch, zeroing in on his location even before he'd spotted him. Above and behind him he felt von Fleiden, outraged, snatching at his wake, then pursuing.

Psychic filaments probed at his mind, looking for a way to pop it loose from its shell. He smelled the Fireman's essence below. Ray forced himself to dive straight toward the slavering murderer, feeling the monster's hungry joy at his approach. If he could manage to fuck the guy up, that might draw off enough of von Fleiden's energy to make her vulnerable. It was the closest thing to a hope he had.

Not very close, really.

As Ray cannonballed down, he spotted the Fireman waiting in a clearing. Near the nude pulsating priapic heap of muscle was a pile of something Ray couldn't identify at first. After a half-second, he managed: naked, mangled corpses. Ray had whetted the Thrall's appetite, and then he'd had to seek satisfaction elsewhere.

Later Ray would wish that his initial reaction had been a rage to get justice for these poor anonymous victims. Instead he felt only bowel-squirting terror.

Ray tried slamming directly into the Fireman with both fists, like something Superman would do to General Zod; the Fireman easily grabbed him by the wrists and used his momentum to flip him into a stand of trees. If not for force-fields that automatically sprouted to encase and cushion his body (some of his training had paid off, at least), Ray would have broken his back along with all his other bones.

Woozily he watched the Fireman advance, slowly, drooling, leering. Behind him von Fleiden descended. She gave no command in words, but Ray could feel a psychic communication passing from her to her Thrall. Although he wasn't privy to its exact words, he could make out its sense well enough: a stern command to the Fireman that he not get too close, that he leave Ray for her. She wasn't taking any more chances of letting her pet be abused by this unpredictable creature. The Fireman stopped but Ray could feel his quivering frustration.

Suddenly rage boiled the wet fear out of Ray's innards. The Fireman wanted to fight? Fuck him, then. Ray brought up his fists and conjured flames, that he poured into the Fireman's face. Again, he had no idea how he did it.

But it was a hell of a lot more heat and power than he'd managed before. And calibrated to a supernatural degree, so that not one spark strayed into the surrounding woods, but all that solar heat plunged into its mark, the Fireman's body, and boiled and melted him from within.

At this onslaught, even more impressive and surprising than his previous two, von Fleiden howled and slapped the air, sending a kinetic blow at Ray that sent him flailing back again onto the ground, cutting off his attack. Gasping for breath, he looked up to see her advancing on him, grimly and no longer at all amused. This was it. She was going to kill him.

Ray knew that the only way he might possibly stay alive was if he could keep on being unpredictable.

Fuck it. He decided to try the Pull'gath.

A brief aside about the Pull'gath.

Untold eons ago, the Old Ones descended to the Earth. This was long before the rise of Man, long before the monstrous sauropods thundered across the land. Before the first cell divided in two in some obscure and briney mud puddle, the Old Ones held their revels under the acid rains and upon the fresh edges of new, still-jagged rock.

Even had human eyes existed in that far-flung age, they would not have been able to truly see the forms of those huge Old Ones, who reflected light in odd and unheard-of fashions. And even had there been eyes which could manage to take in the raw sensory data, no human mind could survive the task of processing it. Human neural pathways would never be able to reconstitute such information. The geometries of the Old Ones were subtler and more grotesque than those of humans (and still are, perhaps—for there are those who claim the Old Ones remain even now, here in our mundane dimension, sleeping dormant under the planet's surface, but destined one day to rise, to break through that surface, and so shatter this petty Creation into a billion delicious darknesses). The sight of an Old One would scramble any human visual cortex. It would drive that poor human into madness, and beyond.

Those Old Ones had revels, but they also had wars. In fact the two were indistinguishable. They fought for stakes no human could understand, under mind-breaking banners. No human tongue could wrap itself around their *noms de guerre*, no human ear contain them. For the most part, the same was true of their tactics. No mere meat mortal could hope to pronounce the names of such tactics, nor comprehend even in broad outlines by what processes such tactics operated.

An exception was the Pull'gath. No one really knows why.

It is not merely that the basic principles of Pull'gath are accessible to human comprehension. It is even possible for a human to master the technique itself, albeit only if that human is a master mage.

Pull'gath is a sort of mystical judo. One takes the thaumaturgical force being hurled at one, and flips it so that it is instead turned against the assailant. A true master can even amplify the force, through the lens of the third eye.

The risk is that the mage attempting Pull'gath does not actually flip the power; the power continues rushing towards the unfortunate mage, only irritated and amplified. Usually this occurs when the mage is inexperienced and untrusting of his own elegance. The mage doesn't trust that a deft psychic motion is all that is needed, and instead tries to add his own force. Such a lack of confidence tends to be disastrous, since the added force gets swallowed up by the oncoming thaumatokinetic blow, adding to it and leaving the would-be practitioner of the technique in straits even more dire than before.

So, this was the move that Ray decided to try on Melania von Fleiden.

Fifteen

A tidal wave was surging behind Melania von Fleiden's brow. Ray couldn't see any sign of it, aside from the rich malevolent excitement in her eyes. But he could hear a rushing sound. And he could feel atoms vibrating all around him.

The natural curves and slants were going out of the trees which bordered the clearing. As if some great magnet in the sky were pulling them up straight. Enough power was building to blast him from existence, like flame through dandelion fluff.

Ray ignored and denied his fear, insisted to himself on his own confidence. In truth, he was relieved that it was von Fleiden he was facing, not the Fireman. He recognized the stupidity of that. Von Fleiden was vastly more formidable than her slave. But the Fireman had beaten a visceral fear into him. Ray couldn't look directly at the throbbing menace of the creature's penis. And, ridiculous as it was, von Fleiden just looked so feminine.

He focused on trying to prep for the Pull'gath. Remembering all the instructions he'd read on the sly, in the books Ned had told him he wasn't ready for yet.

As the power came rushing at him he realized there was no chance he would succeed.

He gave it his all, though. Fear spurred him on. All of Creation was coming at him like a wall at his face, and he let himself tumble with it, kicking out with his mind to send her power flying overhead, too high to catch him, then flipping himself over and whipping out his mental limbs to wrest the power from her and redirect the energy back around, to send her tumbling all the way out of the universe if all went well.

It didn't really go down like that. But it also wasn't a complete failure.

At first Ray had no idea what had happened: neither what had gone wrong, nor what had gone right. He seemed to no longer be in the woods, but even of that he couldn't be sure—everything was flashing lights, exploding color, there was no reliable information coming in from any of his senses. Had he been killed?!

If he had been, then he figured he had brought von Fleiden down with him. He couldn't see her, touch her, or smell her, but he could feel her presence here in this psychedelic void, laughing wrathfully and thrashing around in search of him. Perceiving her raw consciousness this way, without the sight and touch and smell of her, was terrifying; she was stripped of all those aspects he'd been conditioned to find delight in, and only her core was left.

Even that core, though, he found difficult to turn away from. At first he thought it was purely murderous, but then he realized that wasn't true. It was just that right now she really wanted to murder him. But underneath that urge, there were unfathomable depths in which affection, play, greed, fear, and so many other qualities roiled together in a soup of dreams and memory.

In this realm time worked differently, so these reflections of Ray's might have taken a nanosecond or an eon. Then von Fleiden grabbed him.

The formlessness of his mystical body struggled and gasped in that primordial darkness. But there was no escaping her; she had expanded her body so that it encompassed and encased his. Her mystical atoms began to penetrate his own, and with them came a rough understanding of what had happened.

He'd fucked up the Pull'gath. But he had not fucked it up half as disastrously as he might have done. He had managed to partially harness and then redirect the blow von Fleiden had aimed at him. But he had not been able to retain control of it, and von Fleiden had wrested back her power.

That power was again diminished, though. She'd used up a lot of it in the attack she'd aimed at him, and for the moment she no longer had enough to simply vaporize him outright.

That attack had been intended to destroy him. In partially taking control of it, and partially redirecting it toward von Fleiden, Ray had managed to not be disintegrated, but had still been sent to someplace like the void of death, all while dragging von Fleiden along with him.

Here in this quasi-unreal state, the odds should have been somewhat even. Except that von Fleiden was so much more experienced than him. He could hear in the wildness of her angry laughter that she understood that he had attempted Pull'gath on her, and that he'd done better than she would have expected although he'd still failed. In short, she understood a hell of a lot more than he would have in her place, and she also understood how to handle him now.

She was still encasing him. Holding him. He tried to struggle, but it was difficult. It took him a second to realize that he wasn't really trying hard.

It was like she had sent a little dart into the nucleus of each one of his cells. And those darts had hollow points, and they set themselves to sucking at those nuclei. Like snakes inserting their arrow-shaped heads into the white smoothness of eggs and slowly sucking out the yolks. These piercings filled his whole being with countless little pinching pains. They were smoothed over by a sort of sickly pleasure, like lightly spoiled honey, which seemed to mingle with his blood.

His body was being invaded. Taken over. Used. Sucked dry. In a panic he tried to shake loose. Somewhere behind him, von Fleiden grabbed him by something like the spiritual equivalent of the nape of his neck. Murmuring low in his astral ear, she growled at him to relax and enjoy it, and continued piercing him anew. Soon all his vitality would be drained.

Feeling himself drooping into something like sleep, Ray made one more effort to shake her off and get free. It didn't even faze her; she yanked him back against her chest and held fast to him. He felt the strength of her phantom fingers and despaired. There was no way he could break free of that grip.

Fighting to stay awake, as the succubus drained his life-force, he struggled to remember anything from Ned's training that might keep him alive. Perversely, his mind kept trying to turn to a particular issue of *The Fantastic Four* that he had once read. Some infantile part of him must be seeking comfort in childhood memories, during these last few seconds of life. Ray strained to get back on track, to be a sensible grown-up and focus on shit that mattered.

But he couldn't. As his strength drained away, so did his powers of concentration. Finally he found himself dwelling on that random comic book issue, as from a distance the prickling pains of von Fleiden's probings increased.

In that issue the Fantastic Four had come into contact with an alien with a peculiar, perverse power. Instead of fighting loose from the Thing's or Reed Richards's grasp, or trying to bust out of whatever high-tech cage the team stuck him in, this creature used its vibratory powers. This being was able to find the so-called "atomic frequency" of any group of molecules, and adjust its own frequency so that its atoms could slip through any matter. Whatever was trying to constrain him, be it flesh or metal, he could pass through it like smoke, if only he could set himself to vibrate at precisely the correct frequency.

Through all the layers of cottony numbness enwrapping him, Ray began to get excited. Hey, maybe this hadn't been such a random thought after all! All that bunk about vibrating your "atomic frequency" in order to pass through physical objects smelled like bullshit science Stan Lee had dreamt up fifteen minutes before a story deadline. But here on the mystical plane, it sounded pretty solid.

Not that Ray had a clear idea of how to vibrate his atomic frequency so that it matched von Fleiden's. But he gave it a tentative try. At the very least it seemed more feasible than breaking free by brute strength.

He concentrated his attention on his spiritual atoms, those same cells being pierced and sucked upon. If he looked too close at them the pleasure/pain came into sharp focus and, gasping, he had to turn away; but he forced his gaze back upon them. He slowly forced himself to open entirely to the intense sensations he was receiving, to accept and experience them instead of shutting them out. Although time was slipping away, this was not a process that could be rushed. Ray hung there, suspended in the void, eyes closed and mouth open with fear and ecstasy.

Once he had accepted the sensations, once he was no longer trying to push away the transmissions from his atoms, push them away and deny their truth, then it became once again possible to influence them. Tentatively, he tried to move first one, then a few. As long as the atoms weren't trying to push back directly against the pressure being applied by von Fleiden, he could do so; if she were pushing them down, then he could not push them up, but he could move them from side to side. He did so.

Such lateral motion sparked an answering motion from von Fleiden's invading atoms. As Ray's atoms moved, the resistant pressure faced by her atoms changed. The motion this occasioned in her atoms gave Ray clues as to their habitual vibratory patterns.

Clues—but he knew better than to try to analyze them using his intellect. No way would it ever move fast enough. His only hope was to let go of his intentionality, yet still retain control. Like so many paradoxical moves, that required confidence, and a store of previously accumulated discipline and training, that could be drawn on now without recourse to the clumsiness of directed human thought. Ray wasn't sure he had either quality in sufficient measure. But no point in worrying about it now. Either he'd die, or he wouldn't.

He jostled his atoms against von Fleiden's in the manner that felt right.

He couldn't just do what he thought ought to work. Whatever preconceived notions he might have, they were bound to be too crude. Bound to be inexact; bound to be not strongly enough tied to the real flavor of Melania von Fleiden. In order to get the best of her, he had to first open himself to her, become open to the sensation of her, the tendencies and proclivities of the sensual logic of her own essence. To do that he had to allow himself to become yet more vulnerable to her; there was no way to garner such fine perceptions while distracted by his own defenses. He must open himself to her, and he must do so without the enervating accompaniment of fear.

All this might sound like hippie garbage. Well, it's not easy to describe a battle on the non-physical plane.

Ray let go; somehow, he managed to relax. First he formed the strong but calm intention to vibrate in such a way as to disrupt and slip through von Fleiden's control. Once established, Ray let the intention slip from his conscious mind, trusting that it had left a deep enough impression to hold even after he'd removed his attention from it.

It had. As he abandoned planning and preconceived notions, his vibrations became subtler, more responsive. They triggered a response in von Fleiden's astral body. As her countermoves had to grow subtler, themselves, she in turn also had to abandon a large degree of conscious control. Because she hadn't expected Ray to manage much of a fight, she hadn't taken the precaution of forming a strong intention before going on autopilot, an intention strong enough to create an impression that might continue to steer her actions. Lacking such a constraining influence, her astral body began to respond to his in the way that felt most natural.

Soon the molecules were vibrating in true sympathy with each other. This wasn't exactly what Ray had been aiming for—in fact, he'd visualized almost the opposite—his original, admittedly vague idea had been to vibrate his atoms in the opposite rhythm of Melania's, to become a sort of anti-Melania, so that he would be able to slip his atoms in between hers without their ever touching. What he was doing was managing to not get him killed, though, so it must be all right.

The sensations elicited by those complementary vibrations mounted in intensity, mounted and mounted and mounted. Following some instinct, Ray fought the urge to clap his conscious attention back onto the process, so that he could label the sensations: pleasure, or even pain, but *something* at least, one or the other. Instead he let it just happen, let the raw unordered ebbs and surges of feeling squirt up his nerves and drop back down, over and over, higher and higher and lower and lower.

If he'd let his conscious mind rise to the surface he might have given up, since he would have reasoned there was no way he could outlast the more experienced and disciplined von Fleiden. But she broke first. Her rational mind came scrambling back up to the fore, grabbing ahold of the experience they both shared, in a panic to name and thus control it. She named it pleasure. Once she decided for them both that's what it was, it climaxed; like a psychic candy-colored explosion; Ray felt himself flung onto the empty winds of the void, all his cells burst and spent, their broken diaphanous skins voluptuously farting their substance out into the abyss.

Then he felt his body accreting corporeality, and then he was no longer blowing weightless through the void, but falling. That set off an alarm bell in his psyche, and this time it was his turn to send his conscious mind scrambling to the helm before he wound up splattered on something.

The freeway, as it turned out. He landed on his side and tried to scramble upright so as to get his bearings—the rough asphalt and screams of horns and shredding tires clued him in. Approaching headlights blinded him. He rolled to the left, because his body was already leaning that way anyhow. By dumb luck that took him off the road and onto the shoulder; rolling to the right would have put him under an eighteen-wheeler and turned him into spaghetti sauce. He kept rolling, off the shoulder and into the woods. The horns and tire-screeches dissipated as the traffic settled back into its normal throbbing hum.

At least he hadn't dropped from very high in the sky; he was bruised and skinned up, but hadn't broken anything.

Not even on the inside did he feel broken. Ray noted the fact with some degree of surprise. Exhausted, yes; battered, definitely; but the inner wellspring from which his energy and life force flowed was not dammed or blocked or dry, as it had been after the last two times he'd fought the Fireman. Soon he'd be able to fight again. If he had to, he could even do it now. He noted the fact not so much with joy or pride, as with the stunned amazement he'd felt years ago upon seeing the black wires of his first pubes. Had he finally grown into a real mage?

Anyway, he would need to fight again awful damn soon. The reason the cars were using their headlights was that it was night. Maybe that fight had taken longer than he'd thought, or maybe time passed differently on the astral plane. Either way, that Sealing Spell would be expiring soon.

He wasn't broken. Tired, though. And with plenty of wounds to lick. He'd scratched and scraped himself anew when he'd rolled through the brambles and thorn bushes and into the woods, but he barely felt those stings and burnings after the wallop of his fall—too much energy had been drained for him to feel much more than that. Only tatters of his garments had accompanied him through whatever he'd come through; in fact, he realized, these rags were stuck to him solely because of his sweat and blood, and he was basically naked. He kept lying in the dirt and weeds. Normally he would have been more fastidious, more worried about bugs and worms crawling into his hair and into the crevices of his body. Right now, he couldn't care less.

He felt tired, strained, battered. More so than ever before in his life. He felt something else too, though, something to do with von Fleiden, and he tried to hold it still in his mind and look carefully at it till he could name what it was.

After a few minutes, he started to wonder if maybe he didn't kind of love her.

Not that he felt horny for her. All that had evaporated when she'd killed Ned, and Ray, being still young and naive, couldn't imagine that any pheromones or glamour would ever change that. What he felt was deeper, mellower, more melancholy.

Not exactly sexual, but with an erotic element nonetheless. Ray wondered where the hell this feeling had come from; then he realized that, duh, it was thanks to the battle of the vibrating atoms out there on the astral plane.

After all, no experience could possibly create as much sympathy as attuning your very atoms to the vibratory patterns of another's; it literally created sympathy at the atomic level. Love has many provocations and many types, and some of them are tied up with sympathy.

Not a sympathy with her aims or motives, not really. He had no exact knowledge of what those were, other than greed and fear of her client. But he now felt more inclined to judge such motives generously. And he was sure that, if he tried, if he probed his own intuition, he would be able to tease out subtler, more forgivable spurs to her crime. Childhood terrors whose repercussions she could not control, whose very origins were beyond the pale of her knowledge. Dreams which in their pure state had been beautiful but had been twisted out of shape by life's cruel winds.

He felt as if he would be able to forgive her just about anything now. Disturbed, he asked himself the obvious question: even Ned's death? The raw and wounded part of himself where Ned's broken corpse still rested shrank and shrieked at Ray's probing touch. His pain and grief had not lessened. And yet he thought that maybe he didn't quite hate von Fleiden for it anymore.

That realization shamed him. He curled up with it there in the thorny weeds, hiding from the world while he rested, rebuilt his strength, and tried to figure out what to do about this new feeling.

Reluctantly, he reminded himself that he had a deadline. No matter how the astral battle had mucked up his feelings about von Fleiden, he still had to stop her from getting away with those medallions once the Sealing Spell wore off at 5:32. That was his duty.

"Also, my destiny," he muttered, as a tribute to Ned. Even if he did roll his eyes as he said it.

The flow of cars and lights going by was endless and monotonous. Now it took him a second to notice that one had separated itself from the communal noise—an engine came closer than the others, brakes squeaked, he saw the glare of two headlights penetrate the woods at a new angle and then rest there, stationary. A car had pulled over onto the shoulder, just beside him.

All his existential and ethical musings were expelled, under the sudden squeezing pressure of fear. It was hard to imagine Melania von Fleiden coming after him in a car, now that he'd seen her flying. But he had a vision of the Fireman, hunched over the wheel, scowling and squinting into the woods, drooling.

"Ray?!" A quivery voice—Aisha's. "Ray, are you out there?!"

He leapt to his feet and staggered back toward the shoulder. Something cut the sole of his foot and reminded him that his shoes had been pulverized along with his clothes, which reminded him that he was naked. Peering through the branches, he saw Aisha standing next to her parked car. The streaming headlights of the freeway backlit her, but he could still make out her nervous expression because she was holding a glowy something. It was that amulet Ned had given her.

"Aisha?" he called. "I'm over here."

Relieved, she took a step toward his voice, but then frowned. "Why don't you come out where I can see you?"

"Um, I…. What're you doing here, anyway? How'd you know I was here?"

She raised the amulet. "I told you. Ned gave me this, so that I'd be able to find you if you were in trouble. It shines when it gets near you."

Ray flushed. God damn it! Aisha was a mere mortal with no magic powers—if anyone should be defending someone, it should be *him* defending *her*!

"How'd you even know I was in trouble?" he demanded.

"Obviously you were in trouble. So I've been driving around all day waiting for this thing to glow."

At the idea of her driving around for hours looking for him, Ray felt moved, embarrassed, and guilty. Gas was not cheap.

In any case, it was out of the question that he let Aisha see him nude. "Thanks, but I'm doing okay, actually." He tried to say it with such easy nonchalance that she would be convinced.

"*Get* your skinny little ass in my car!" barked Aisha. "Ned said to look after you and I'll be god-damned if I'm not gonna do it!"

Cowed, Ray picked his way gingerly through the stickers and sharp pebbles. Aisha waited for him with a stern glare and her fists on her hips. When he finally stepped out into the light of the freeway, sheepishly cupping his penis and testicles in one hand and fanning the other hand behind him to cover his butt-crack, she blanched. "Jesus Christ," she muttered. On the verge of opening the passenger door for him, she hesitated; both of them froze a moment, thinking about the awkwardness of his bare ass on her upholstery. But they had shit to do, plus some passing motorist was bound to notice the naked half-Asian boy and the plump black woman and decide that was so unusual that someone ought to call the police about it. After they'd been in the car a few minutes and had time to get used to Ray's nakedness, it struck them both as weird that they'd hesitated over something so petty. The embarrassment over that hesitation, not the nudity itself, was why they avoided referring to it. Aisha stopped at Ned's house along the way, without comment, so that Ray could grab some clothes.

Sixteen

Along the way to where? Ray had been so tamed by Aisha's outburst on the freeway shoulder that he didn't even ask till after he'd put on clothes and Aisha was reversing out of Ned's driveway. Once he heard the answer he reverted to form, flying into a tizzy and repeating words like "never," "no way," and "are you crazy?"

"She can help," said Aisha, exasperated. This was the first time she'd ever had to wrangle Ray—that had always been Ned's job. "She knows more about this stuff than anybody else in town that *I* know of. Do *you* know anybody else?"

"Britney totally got Ned killed! Doesn't that mean anything to you?!"

"I don't really think it was that simple!" Aisha spoke almost in a wail, her voice infused with all the tears she refused to cry. Ray shut up. He settled back in his seat; if Aisha wanted to try to enlist the Oracle's aid, fine. It wasn't as if he had better ideas.

Besides, it was bullshit that Britney had gotten Ned killed. Ray just wanted to duck his own responsibility—Ned had died to protect *him*.

"Buckle your seatbelt," said Aisha, the words still thick with choked-down grief. Ray obeyed, absently.

Absent in part because he was embarrassed by his outburst. But only in part. He was thinking. When he'd been thrust back onto the physical plane, when he'd lain down naked in the nettles and pored over the odd change in his feelings for von Fleiden as his blood dried and his sweat cooled, he'd taken for granted that the battle had effected some great change in his inmost being, as well. But the little outburst he'd just had made it seem obvious that he remained the same guy, after all.

Well, he definitely had that guy in him, the guy he'd always been. But as he let himself grow quiet again, he once more felt that he had something new within him, as well. Something mellower, something sadder. Something that he thought just possibly might be wiser, because it seemed more willing than his normal self to admit it had no clue what was going on.

They pulled over to the curb in front of Britney's house. The manner in which Aisha overcame her obvious reluctance in order to lift herself out of the car and civilly approach the house set a good example for Ray.

Britney came to the front door to meet them, leaning her shoulder against the frame, arms crossed over her chest. Trying too hard to look relaxed. She and Aisha exchanged slight, fraught nods, which would have been enough to let Ray know if he hadn't already that they'd met earlier and talked things over. The cats rushed him, then stopped a foot away, encircling him and sniffing. He didn't know if they were singling him out because they remembered his earlier violence, or because Britney had told them to keep their eyes on him, or because they were attracted to the stink of his dried blood.

As he neared the well-lit patio, Britney did a double-take. "You lost your cherry," she said to him.

He nearly tripped on the way up her porch steps. "What does that mean?" he stammered.

Britney smirked. "You know."

Indeed, he kinda-sorta did. Something to do with the new emotions he felt about Melania von Fleiden. On a different note, he couldn't help but be reminded of that first threat the Fireman had made to him. There was still time for the Thrall to make good on it.

They followed Britney into the house. Instead of clearing enough cats off the sofas and chairs to sit in the living room like normal people, they followed her into the hallway, with its troughs and jumbo bags of cat food. There the Oracle stood in her sea of fur and got back to her eternal toil of ripping open the bags and pouring the dry pellets out for her minions.

"Can I give you a hand?" asked Aisha, not sounding like she really wanted to. She had to raise her voice to be heard over the tinny thunder of the hard pellets pouring into the trough. This one was aluminum.

Britney shook her head impatiently. Once she'd served up her own body weight in food, she straightened and said, "Follow me. We're low on time." As they proceeded further into the house she crumpled the bag into a manageable bundle. The crumpling was loud, the meowing cats were loud. It would drive him nuts to live here, Ray decided.

They went into her bedroom. The bed was covered with lounging cats who looked up sharply at the entrance of their mistress, then settled down again when she issued no commands. While Britney dug around for something on the top shelf of her closet (she had to stand on two stacked, battered, and precarious-looking cardboard boxes to reach it), Ray eyed the bed with discreet curiosity. Britney and ol' Ned must have done the deed there. He carefully avoided looking at Aisha.

Britney found whatever she was looking for and jumped down, nearly spilling onto her rump in the process—whatever qualities she might share with her billions of cats, grace was not among them. With her left hand she pushed her hair out of her face, with her right she handed Ray some kind of necklace. "Here," she said. "Wear this, and you might have a chance."

"Really?" snapped Aisha, suspicious. "I thought when we talked before you said you didn't have any charms or amulets or anything strong enough to do any good against this Melania von Fleiden woman. I thought you said the best you could do was just talk over strategies with Ray."

This necklace didn't look like much. Neither did its charm. It was a rock, as far as Ray could tell. Like, a little gray smooth rock shaped sort of like a doggy treat, roughly cylindrical with two fat knobby ends, with a black thread tied around its skinny middle, a black thread which also formed the necklace itself. As a trained mage—or, well, an apprentice mage—he knew perfectly well that looks could be deceiving. Still, what this necklace looked like was just a regular old rock.

Britney nodded through Aisha's objections. Her eyes stayed on Ray. "That was all true, then. But von Fleiden's weaker now. Weak enough that this amulet might give Ray just enough protection, at the critical moment."

"What made her so weak all of a sudden?" demanded Aisha.

"Same thing that made Ray weaker." Just as he was about to make an annoyed comment about her speaking of him in the third person while looking him in the eye, she addressed him directly: "I honestly never would have thought you'd have the stuff for a move like that. The Pull'gath, but also whatever happened in the astral plane. Some of Ned's emotional intelligence must have rubbed off on you after all."

He turned red. He was certain she was referring to the new, strange feeling he had about von Fleiden; he hadn't decided whether or not the feeling constituted a betrayal of Ned, and regardless he didn't want anyone to know about it. "I don't know what you're talking about." How had the cats been able to tell her about the Pull'gath, anyway?

She snorted. "Learn not to blush if you want to keep secrets. I may not have my cats posted in the Void That Lies Between Worlds, but I can read your face well enough to know what happened there."

Ray could see Aisha becoming impatient and confused. To head off her questions, he said, "So this little rock really isn't just a little rock?"

"It may not look like much," said the Oracle. "But it can pack quite a kick. All depends what you bring to it. And that makes it a double-edged sword. The emotions in the air, the intentions, the actions even—the amulet picks them up and amplifies them. If two people confront each other in its presence, and their emotions are in synch anyway, the amulet can stimulate a powerful feedback loop between them. Might overwhelm both players. Might even prevent any violence, period."

100

Aisha frowned. "Why would von Fleiden's and Ray's feelings being amplified *prevent* violence? They hate each other, don't they?"

Ray blushed. "Nothing's gonna prevent the violence," he muttered.

Britney shrugged. "Anyway. If anyone does commit violence, the amulet will amplify that, as well, right there on the physical plane—so be careful. An emotional feedback loop might level the playing field. Will that let you defeat her? I don't know, that depends on you. No one can predict how shit like this'll play out till after the battle's done." Then she added, "The amulet's most effective against lovers."

It was obvious the Oracle had thrown that in to make Ray squirm. Aisha shot him a look of shocked disgust; Ray wondered if she thought Britney meant he and von Fleiden were literally lovers, as in they'd had sex. Redder than ever, he said, "Why exactly should we trust you, anyway? I mean, you basically sent Ned out to get killed."

Britney's face was like a bear trap snapping shut, and also like the limb it was snapping shut upon. She turned her back on them both. At first Ray wondered why, then felt impossibly dense as he realized it was to hide her tears. "You'd better go, asshole," she said, still hiding her face. "You've got an appointment. And I've got to keep feeding all these damn cats."

Ray felt ashamed, again. He'd only said that to hurt her, because he was mad about the "lovers" comment.

When they were in the yard, almost at Aisha's car, they heard the Oracle call to them from the front door: "Good luck! Let me know how it all turns out."

Seventeen

In a cave on the side of a hill outside Sallisburg, whose vine-clogged entrance would be all but invisible to any hiker or hunter finding himself this far from any trail, Melania von Fleiden wasted time drawing power from the biosphere to knit the flesh and spirit of her once-more-broken Thrall.

She ought to leave him to die, she told him, since he was too weak to defeat the boy and too dumb to comprehend that fact. It was true, but she didn't mean it. She tried to convince him that she did, though, so as to get him to stay the fuck out of it next time.

From his psychic moans of grief, it would seem he was convinced. Good. Von Fleiden wasted no sorrow on his mere emotional pain. She cared for her Thrall enough to want to keep him alive, but that didn't mean she was utterly soft.

Her palm rested on his sticky forehead. Not to show tenderness, but because the palm was the channel via which the biosphere's energy entered her Thrall, lending him strength to heal. But in the red-rimmed, wild, adoring eyes that stared up at her, begging forgiveness, one could see that he took it for tenderness and was grateful. Well, she would not begrudge him that.

All his suffering was her own fault. Firstly, because she was the leader and ultimately responsible for everything, period. Buck stopped with her. But even putting that aside, it should have been predictable that the creature that had once been Steve Blevins would continue to rush into danger, would be incapable of learning moderation.

Their first meeting replayed itself in her mind's eye. She maintained her stern expression, lest the Thrall should doubt her seriousness, but it was hard not to laugh with rueful affection.

It happened back when Steve Blevins was a real fireman. An enchantment of Melania's had set alight the dilapidated building she'd happened to occupy. The flames had been the last step of that particular mission, and there had been no reason for her not to slip through a dimensional portal and be on her way. But she'd paused to exult and delight in the fire. And she'd been there, booming full-throated laughter in the middle of a room where the flames licked at her without ever quite touching the skin, when Blevins had burst through the door. A simple fireman, come to fight a fire.

In any case, that's what he'd been when he entered. He wasn't that by the time he left. Maybe he stopped being that the moment he lay eyes on von Fleiden. For the truth is, that was when he'd become her Thrall. Her own sorcery was merely secondary. That was just what kept him alive.

He, mere mortal, had seen her and known right away what she was. That touched von Fleiden more than anything (what she experienced as "being touched" was a type of surprised, gentle amusement); right away, her own senses and expertise had clued her in that Blevins had no psychic sensitivity to speak of. Nor brains. And yet he really had known what she was. Despite having no cause to believe in magic, he'd known her for a sorceress; and he'd thrown down his axe and gone to his knees before her on the burning floor.

Laughing, she'd asked him with her mind if he realized he was about to be burned alive.

Also speaking silently, he'd replied that he knew she could save him if she wished, and that his life was hers to do with as she wished; he was in love with her.

Her surprised, gentle laughter grew stronger. Just to see if he really meant it, if he truly would let himself be burned to death rather than leave her side, she waited till the fire took its first blistering bite at him. Then she swept him up in her arms, took him, changed him, improved him, Enthralled him. Now he was her faithful servant. And she resolved to stay his faithful mistress, in return.

She thought of the Takeshi boy and forced her mouth to twist with contempt. What a contrast he made with her Fireman! And yet she couldn't fool herself into believing in that contempt. True, there seemed to be something flimsy and weak in the boy's constant doubts, when one compared them to her Thrall's limitless and spontaneous faith. Yet weren't those doubts born of his restless, questioning, orphaned spirit? That spirit had its own strange and exasperating but true beauty.

Von Fleiden was no fool. Even better than Takeshi, she knew what had happened, what he'd inadvertently accomplished in that dance of atoms. Now she was stuck loving the little bastard, after her fashion. Killing him would be like chewing off a limb. Couldn't be helped, though. She'd tasted his contours, and come to feel a sad kinship with his fears. And even without the influence of that supernatural event, she might have started to feel a soft spot for his jittery brand of courage.

Didn't matter. If he wouldn't give up, she'd kill him. She repeated that to herself, made herself face the prospect head-on.

She told herself that she was a hard-ass bitch who'd already chewed off plenty of limbs in her time and could do it again if need be. And that wasn't bullshit.

From his thick gray fog of pain her Fireman sent up a mental wail, a foghorn to let her know he was there, ready to serve.

Von Fleiden sent him calming waves in response.

Instead of letting himself be calmed, though, he began to squander what strength she'd restored to him in an access of rage. Visions popped into her mind, of Ray Takeshi's burst and oozing body. She didn't conjure them—her Thrall was spitting them out with such force she couldn't help but see. Hiding from him the pain such images caused (it would have been a cruel, needless insult to let him know she had come to feel this way for their nemesis, that she had been more intimate with him than she and her Thrall ever had), she scolded him. Scolded him hard enough to make him flinch.

He was *not* to meddle! He had proven his pathetic unworthiness multiple times! She forbade him to make a fool of himself and of her yet again!

He had no real teeth to gnash—they had burst in the force and heat of Takeshi's attack, and were mere jagged nubs. But he made a raggedy wet noise of agony in his throat.

She smirked at his pain. It might be true that she was a kind mistress, but only relative to the normal relations between others of her kind and their Thralls. The proof of her affection was that she did not smite him, or simply leave him to die and waste no more power on him.

Yet the affection was real. Without letting him know, not allowing him to sense they came from her (for it suited her purposes for him to think her wrathful), she sent more soothing waves to him. And she told him (almost without noticing herself that her tone had grown gentler) that anyway, he would be too weak to even survive another encounter with the boy. She could only restore him to the strength of a mortal man, and a wounded one at that. He would have no more than the mundane capabilities of the Steve Blevins he'd once been—less, thanks to his madness. He would only get in her way.

He howled in shame. She turned away from him, tragically underestimating how sharp the goad of his wounded pride would prove to be.

No daylight at all seeped through the curtain of vines and brambles that hid the cave mouth. Night. Time to leave her Fireman behind, and venture out to the bus depot, to the medallions, to the battle.

Briefly she daydreamed of making the Takeshi boy her Thrall, as well. Two Thralls would be a serious drain, and it would probably be a long while before they accepted each other as brothers. She thought she might be able to try it, though.

But who was she kidding? When she'd met the boy, he'd been open to seduction. But not now, not even taking into account this feeling which had been engendered in them both. No, she reflected, with heavy regret; no, she was probably going to have to kill him.

Eighteen

Hard to believe, but there was nothing left but for Aisha to drive him back to that bus depot and drop him off, like a mom dropping her kid off for the first leg of his school trip. Except instead of a school trip he was being dropped off for mortal combat, probable death, and possible pre-death rape and dismemberment.

They didn't talk during the drive. Absently Ray fingered the rock that hung around his neck. It did have a charge, but it really did not feel like much at all, and he had a hard time believing the pebble was going to do him any good.... Oh, well. Maybe von Fleiden wouldn't risk her Thrall on him again. Maybe she'd just annihilate him with a blast of her power. Ray wasn't suicidal—but he was so tired that the idea of sleeping for all eternity didn't strike him as particularly nightmarish right now.

Except that wasn't an option. If von Fleiden delivered those medallions, untold evil might be caused—Ned had said so. He couldn't just lay down and die, because that would be letting Ned down.

He knew that if Ned were alive and could hear this reasoning, he would frown with patient annoyance and point out that Ray's prevention of the delivery should have nothing to do with Ned; Ray should do it in order to prevent evil from being inflicted upon whomever it was going to be inflicted upon.

I know I should be doing it for all those innocent strangers, thought Ray. *But I'm doing it for you anyway, Ned.*

While they were still a quarter-mile off from the gleaming oasis of the bus depot, Ray said, "Here's fine." He worked hard to keep his voice from trembling, but was still surprised when it didn't.

Aisha was nervous. She stopped the car, but said, "Are you sure? I could bring you in closer...."

"Don't worry. I'll walk. You can go home—I'll call you when I'm done." Even that, he managed to say with a level tone, despite how preposterous it seemed to think he would be anything but dead in an hour.

Aisha was shaking her head: "No. I'm gonna wait right here."

"Don't, Aisha. You've already done everything you can, but the rest of this is all magic stuff. You can't help. Go home. That's what Ned would want. Go home and get the kiln fired up, so I can destroy these medallions."

Her mouth pressed itself into a tight, frustrated line, but she knew he was right. "I'll wait for you at Ned's house," she said. "Now you go kick these people's ass. That's what Ned would want, too."

"Okay."

He got out of the car and watched Aisha drive away. There was no other traffic on the dark two-lane highway. No other sign of habitation anywhere, except for the gleaming depot. It felt eerie. The buzz of cicadas carpeted everything.

Ray had wondered if he would really have the balls to return to the scene of his trouncing. But he found his sneakered feet slapping their way softly in that direction. He pulled his phone out of his pocket and checked the time. 5:03—only half an hour till the Sealing Spell dissolved. He wondered if von Fleiden and the Fireman would show up right on time, or if they'd already be there waiting to meet him.

Stepping through the automatic sliding glass door, he saw no sign of his enemies. There were, however, eight homeless people lounging, slouching, dozing on benches. From the smell he was sure they were homeless. Ray thought it would be hard to sleep on these narrow plastic benches, but he supposed it beat the side of the road. Anyway, he had to clear them out before the big battle, so he went to each elderly heap of clothes and flesh (although most were less elderly than he'd first thought), gingerly shaking him or her, and saying, "Excuse me, sir," or "ma'am," as the case might be, "but you can't stay here. There's about to be some trouble." It was hard to touch the first one, what with the smell and the grime, but by number eight it wasn't so bad. There was lots of grumbling, but none of the arguing or swearing or craziness Ray had been worried about. He didn't think he looked particularly impressive, but the homeless people seemed to take him for some sort of legitimate authority figure. Maybe they'd been conditioned to take orders from just anybody.

His first fifteen minutes were taken up with herding these people out into the night—even the most docile of them moved slowly, and he had to spend time hemming and hawing with those who wanted to know where they ought to go sleep instead (Sallisburg did have a homeless shelter, but the buses didn't run at night so how would they get there?). Only as the eighth and final derelict was shuffling her way through the exit did Ray spot von Fleiden. She'd found a bit of shadow to lounge in. As the final homeless lady departed von Fleiden pushed herself off the wall, hands in the pockets of her bright-red pantsuit, and strolled in Ray's direction with a mocking smile. "Well, well, well." Her hair was platinum blonde now. Ray figured she'd changed it to go better with the red pantsuit, which made her look smokin'. "What a good Samaritan."

Ray managed not to retreat in fear before her. On the other hand, when he tried to come up with some repartée, all he managed was, "Oh, you know. Not really."

Her mocking smile didn't alter. Still moving toward him, slowly, she said, "Why don't you let that be your good deed for the day? Don't overreach."

Again he tried to think of something witty to say. But then he quit trying. "I can't let you take those medallions."

"Correction: you can't *stop* me from taking them. I understand that you're trying to follow in your mentor's footsteps. But perhaps you should remember where those footsteps ended."

The reminder of Ned's murder provoked a predictable spurt of rage. But something else occurred to him, too: von Fleiden was trying to warn him off.

That thing that had happened to him on the astral plane had happened to her, too. A two-way street. Worth remembering.

As she moseyed toward him, he began to move; not in retreat, but toward the spot under the bench where he knew the medallions to be concealed. "I guess if you decide to kill me like you did Ned, I'll just have to try my best to stay alive."

Her smile curdled and ceased to be convincing as she changed her trajectory to head him off. "You're the only one with a decision left to make, boy." She took her hands out of her pockets. He could sense invisible force gathering at the ends of her curled fingers. "I've made a contract. A binding one. If I have to, I'll do you like I did that Child Eater."

"But I'm not like the Child Eater. Am I?" He resisted the urge to finger the amulet around his neck. Hopefully it was manipulating von Fleiden's emotions in his favor; if so, he didn't want to draw her attention to the process.

Judging by the grim set of her jaw, any positive emotions she might feel weren't going to matter. She looked like a true hard-ass. "No," she said, "you're not like the Child Eater. But I'll do you like I did her, even so."

Mere minutes remained until the Sealing Spell wore off. Once that happened they would have to try to kill each other. Ray was hyper-aware of the violent potential building up around von Fleiden. He remembered what the Oracle had said, about how the amulet amplified the emotions and the actions around it. Would he be inviting his own destruction if he tried to answer her violence with his own? Should he be trying some kind of Buddhistic spirit-judo on her? Even if he had the potential to be stronger than von Fleiden, he doubted he could match her without lots of training. Beating a brute like the Thrall with a blast of sheer panic-spurred force was one thing. Von Fleiden, though, was a cool-headed expert mage.

The amulet hanging at his collarbone wasn't doing anything, exactly. Wasn't changing temperature, or glowing, or any of that stuff. Nevertheless Ray was aware of it, as if the little stone were bending the space in its vicinity, as if there were a little patch in the universe there at his chest which sounds couldn't escape from, but stayed tucked up into the space there. Its absence created a compensating hum in his mind. He had no idea whether that was good or bad.

Breath heaved its way in and out of his lungs. His eyes started to sting and his lips started to swell with a strange yearning: to go to von Fleiden, take her in his arms, murmur to her that it was foolish of them to fight, that he was sorry for the way everything had gone down, that they ought to stop and cool their heads and figure a way out of this before something horrible happened.

Bullshit sorcery, he told himself. But not cast by her. Looking into her eyes, with the aid of the insight he'd gleaned from their time on the astral plane, he read the same longing emanating from her. This was *his* doing—first, with the Pull'gath, and now by wearing this amulet into the arena. What he was feeling was that amplification the Oracle had promised, of his own feelings but with the effect compounded by von Fleiden's matching ones. Some of the desire and love he felt was that which originated from within himself, for her; but much of it was not his emotion at all—it was what *she* felt, for him.

And it was potent. Maybe the amulet was amplifying it, but Ray could tell that the raw stuff dwarfed the emotion he'd generated. Perhaps that was because von Fleiden's race felt things more deeply than humans did. Perhaps it was simply because she was older than Ray and her heart had had time to deepen. Or perhaps she was just bigger-souled than him. It wasn't that the feelings flowing from her were so different from those Ray reciprocated with; it was just that there was *more* of them.

Ray couldn't believe he was still willing to fight von Fleiden, still able to resist the tug of the emotion rising out of himself but more especially out of her. Would von Fleiden be able to keep her strength up, as well? After all, these emotions were even stronger for her. Then again, Ray bet it would be unwise to bet against her willpower.

Something moved at the entrance to the depot—the Thrall! Even after Ray had swung his eyes over to the guy, it took a split-second to recognize him—this last day had taken its toll on the Thrall, and he was *diminished* in some not-quite-definable way. Since the Fireman kept tripping her up, Ray was surprised von Fleiden had allowed him a piece of the action this time. Then he caught her look of exasperated fury and realized she hadn't, that the Fireman was violating her orders....Jeez, these Thralls really struck Ray as more trouble than they were worth.

Barely had he made this observation when he saw the slave raise a gun. He must be truly weakened, to resort to such mundane means. The muzzle flashed.

Did the violence unleashed by the Fireman amplify that which Ray instinctively answered with, reinforcing the strength of his blow? In retrospect he would decide it must have. In the moment he had no time to think about it; he only struck.

Only later would he realize that the bullet might have killed him, since he devoted too much strength to counterattack and too little to warding. What saved him was von Fleiden's intervention. With a wave of her hand she made the bullet swerve away from him. Not having time to think was why he failed to redirect the bullet's path; she had unthinkingly diverted it for the same reason.

Anyway, her intervention allowed him to unload his stores on the Fireman.

The hulk twisted and screamed in the red lightning pounding into him from Ray's splayed fingers. Soon he was on fire.

"No!" An invisible something tackled Ray and knocked him against the wall, like he'd been attacked by a two-ton pillow. Von Fleiden raced to her Thrall, whose flames she'd already extinguished. "Can't you do what I say, you fool?!"

The Fireman howled pathetically in reply. Already she was kneeling by his side, her hands on his crisped chest, her anger not able to crowd the tenderness out of her face as she poured into him her curative waves.

She loved that Thrall, Ray realized. He'd known it before, but now it really hit him. Love in a creature as capable as von Fleiden of such casual brutality might seem perverse, but he remembered what he'd read in Ned's dossiers about the emotional terrain of such creatures, their monsoons and droughts, their heights and depths. Von Fleiden loved her loyal pet. And she loved Ray, too. And for that reason she wouldn't want to choose between them. She was hoping to scare him off without killing him. The love she felt for them both was the reason she was using valuable energy trying to heal the Thrall, instead of to kill Ray.

Problem was, he loved her too. And the sympathy he felt for her suddenly made him see even the Fireman in a different light. He could imagine the pain he would feel by proxy upon the hulk's death, and he felt for a moment like he would be willing to let the monster go on living, if only von Fleiden would swear to keep him on a short leash.

A flash in the corner of his eye. He looked over; under the bench was a black sack. The medallions. The Spell had expired.

He unleashed upon the prone Thrall and kneeling von Fleiden all the destructive power he could muster.

The red of the bolts pouring from his hands overpowered the white fluorescents. Underfoot the linoleum buckled and melted. The flames leaping from his hands swallowed the oxygen in the room, but the roar of air rushing in to replace it couldn't drown out the Thrall's howls of agony or von Fleiden's of rage and sorrow.

Only her impulse to save the Thrall and her reluctance to kill Ray had kept him alive. Von Fleiden was still the stronger of the two, and once she overcame her reservations as he had his, he was a goner.

Then he felt something click behind his breastbone. Maybe it was spurred on by this moment's stress and need; maybe the proper time had simply arrived, as Ned had always said it someday would. Whyever it happened, Ray knew instantly what that feeling meant: he had the power. The full power, at last, and at will. The power that had always been his Destiny.

He unleashed it on his enemies, trying to shut the door to his heart.

Almost without noticing it, he directed the bulk of his attack at the Thrall, not von Fleiden. But she placed herself between his bolts and the Fireman, trying to take the brunt of the attack. "Stop!" she cried. "Leave him be!"

Ray ignored her. Finally she realized that, even if he had been endowed with the same unwanted sympathy as her, he was ignoring it. So she did too, counterattacking, matching his savagery. Only it was too late. She was too drained to kill him, now that he'd emerged from his chrysalis. She'd lost too much energy in sustaining the first part of his attack, and in defending and, before that, partially healing her Thrall.

"Stop, damn you!" He wasn't sure if he could actually make out those words over the shrieking wind and flame, or if he simply knew that must be what her twisting mouth said. It was a cry of betrayal; and, although a shameful little-boy part of Ray wanted to protest that he couldn't very well betray her when they'd never had any agreement and she'd tried to kill him several times in the last twenty-four hours, the new part of him, the part that had emerged from that battle of the sympathetic atoms, knew such a claim would be bullshit. That battle had created a natural affinity between them. And while sparing von Fleiden and her Thrall would have been a betrayal to Ned and the forces of Light, what he did now was nevertheless a betrayal too.

He kept on betraying her, pouring fire into the Thrall, overpowering her wards and her desperate healing, till some subtle something made him realize that the Thrall was dead. He cut off his attack. Smoke and the hiss of bubbling plastic filled the room; otherwise there was only the moaning of von Fleiden. Ray tried to catch his breath, his eyes and mouth wide, icy vomit tickling low in his belly and threatening to rise; he'd never killed a human being before, or anything that had once been human.

Von Fleiden's moans began to deepen and roughen into a growl. Without hesitation Ray opened up the floodgates of his newfound power, this time slamming it into her.

He reckoned they might be evenly matched now, all things being equal. But all things were not equal. Melania had just wasted a huge quantity of her reserves in defending her Thrall. If she hadn't hesitated, if she'd gone for Ray's throat at the very beginning, before the Thrall had ever come in, she probably could have taken him.

But she hadn't. And now he reckoned he could kill her, if he kept pounding at her like this.

And pound he did. Killing her was the right thing to do. What Ned would call the lesser evil. It wasn't like she was going to find a new line of work. If he let her go, she would be smuggling something else across interdimensional lines tomorrow, something just as malignant as the medallions of Skarth.

But that sickly feeling overcame him. He rocked on his feet, and finally had to cut off the spigot of flame, before its recoil knocked him over backwards. Smoke obscured his view of Melania prone beside the Fireman's charred corpse. Her own flesh bubbled and melted, but it was already setting itself back into place and re-firming. Healing spells like that cost an experienced mage little energy. They were only a matter of persuading forms to return to their natural patterns.

"Why don't you finish me?" she snarled up at him, still too weak to rise.

"I don't want to kill you," he said. Half-defiantly, half-defensively.

"And here I thought you were a real man. What? Going soft already?"

Ray walked to the sack of medallions, then hesitated. He didn't want to carry them off in von Fleiden's magic sack; if he kept an object endowed by her with enchantment, she might conceivably be able to strike at him through it, remotely. But what else to put them in? If he went off to look for a backpack, who would guard von Fleiden and keep her from nabbing the coins? Luckily he noticed that one of the homeless people had left behind a filthy tote bag filled with aluminum cans. He dumped the cans out and began scooping the gold pieces into it.

"It'll take you an hour or two to recover," he told von Fleiden as he worked, hoping that was true. He couldn't bear to look at her. "By that time these'll already be destroyed, so you don't need to bother coming for them."

"Oh, I won't be back right away," she gasped through the pain of her reknitting flesh. "I'll take my time. Prepare. Plan. And then I'll be back."

"I hope you'll be careful." There were a lot of medallions, but he'd nearly gotten them all into the tote. "I know that client is going to be after you. I wish there was something I could do about that, but there isn't."

"Don't worry about me, boy. You know that saying, there's a thin line between love and hate? You're going to find out how true it is."

Ray didn't answer, and von Fleiden didn't say anything more. He finished shoveling the medallions into the tote, picked it up with a grunt, and used his cell phone to call a taxi. Then he went outside to wait for it, still without looking directly at the battered von Fleiden or the murdered Thrall. Sallisburg was a small town and it took forty minutes for the cab to get there. It was probably the only one on-duty.

Nineteen

The cab dropped him off at Ned's. In the split-second before Ray reached into his pocket it occurred to him that his wallet had been blown to smithereens along with his earlier outfit. Aisha's car was in the driveway, though; while the cabbie waited Ray went inside and sheepishly asked for the fare. She handed him thirty bucks from her purse. Ray paid the cabbie and told him to keep the change, not out of generosity but because he was too exhausted to wait for it.

Back inside, Aisha wanted to know how it had gone. Ray told her that he'd beaten them both, but didn't go into details; he didn't mention that he'd left von Fleiden still alive. He hefted the tote bag and told Aisha he'd be happy to tell her everything, but for now he had to dispose of these medallions; they were malignant. He could feel the mirthless smirking bitter hate emanating off the coins like fumes.

Despite her lack of any great degree of psychic sensitivity, even Aisha seemed affected by the evil of the medallions. Or else she simply knew that Ned would have wanted them destroyed ASAP; whatever the reason, she nodded. For a moment they just stood there. Ray had a depressing premonition of the two of them ceasing to know each other. They'd keep in touch a while, till the searing grief for Ned began to fade. They'd bump into each other sometimes around Sallisburg and always say hello, and maybe stop to chat. But the link between them had been Ned. As his presence faded from their lives, whatever relationship they had would fade as well.

Ray trudged down the steps into the cellar, to Ned's kiln. Aisha had gotten it going, as he'd asked. It was hot.

Ranged along the walls upon shelves were Ned's figurines and statuettes. Ray studied them. Unglazed, unbeautiful, they had no aesthetic qualities that justified their continued existence beyond Ned's life. They were only tools that Ned had produced for the sake of his terramancy. Now that he was gone, there was no one who knew how to use them, and no reason to keep them around.

Not that Ray planned on smashing them, or anything. He surveyed the rows of ugly clay dwarves, trying to pick out the one that had clued Ned in to his upcoming death. They all looked basically the same to him.

Ned had said love was the key. That must have been what his dream-parents had been talking about. Kind of weird that he'd apparently meant the path to manhood would lie through inspiring mutual love, and then totally ignoring it.

His manhood, Ned had said. Ray had assumed that meant growing up, taking responsibility, being an adult, so on and so forth. But maybe Ned had just meant this dryness in the sinuses, this dryness in the heart. So unlike the feminine ebb and swell of von Fleiden's uncontrollable, volcanic passion.

Or maybe that was bullshit. Ned had been a man, and he hadn't been like that ... had he? Maybe Ray was just pussying out as usual, making excuses for his own weak-ass soul.

Maybe. He didn't know. He shoveled the medallions into the kiln, watched them all melt into a lump. Watched as whatever was wild in them burned and drifted away with the smoke.

STEWART AND JEAN, by J. Boyett

A blind date between Stewart and Jean explodes into a confrontation from the past when Jean realizes that theirs is not a random meeting at all, but that Stewart is the brother of the man who once tried to rape her.

THE LITTLE MERMAID: A HORROR STORY,
by J. Boyett

Brenna has an idyllic life with her heroic, dashing, lifeguard boyfriend Mark. She knows it's only natural that other girls should have crushes on the guy. But there's something different about the young girl he's rescued, who seemed to appear in the sea out of nowhere—a young girl with strange powers, and who will stop at nothing to have Mark for herself.

I'M YOUR MAN, by F. Sykes

It's New York in the 1990's, and every week for years Fred has cruised Port Authority for hustlers, living a double life, dreaming of the one perfect boy that he can really love. When he meets Adam, he wonders if he's found that perfect boy after all … and even though Adam proves to be very imperfect, and very real, Fred's dream is strengthened to the point that he finds it difficult to awake.

BENJAMIN GOLDEN DEVILHORNS, by Doug Shields

A collection of stories set in a bizarre, almost believable universe: the lord of cockroaches breathes the same air as a genius teenage girl with a thing for criminals, a ruthless meat tycoon who hasn't figured out that secret gay affairs are best conducted out of town, and a telepathic bowling ball. Yes, the bowling ball breathes.

RICKY, by J. Boyett

Ricky's hoping to begin a new life upon his release from prison; but on his second day out, someone murders his sister. Determined to find her killer, but with no idea how to go about it, Ricky follows a dangerous path, led by clues that may only be in his mind.

BROTHEL, by J. Boyett

What to do for kicks if you live in a sleepy college town, and all you need to pass your courses is basic literacy? Well, you could keep up with all the popular TV shows. Or see how much alcohol you can drink without dying. Or spice things up with the occasional hump behind the bushes. And if that's not enough you could start a business....

THE VICTIM (AND OTHER SHORT PLAYS),
by J. Boyett

In The Victim, April wants Grace to help her prosecute the guys who raped them years before. The only problem is, Grace doesn't remember things that way.... Also included:
A young man picks up a strange woman in a bar, only to realize she's no stranger after all;
An uptight socialite learns some outrageous truths about her family;
A sister stumbles upon her brother's bizarre sexual rite;
A first date ends in grotesque revelations;
A love potion proves all too effective;
A lesbian wedding is complicated when it turns out one bride's brother used to date the other bride.

Made in the USA
Columbia, SC
21 November 2021

49004457R00072